Christian's Look Back at Life

A Christian Fiction Novella on Life and Death

James Bonk

Storming Strongholds LLC

This book is a work of fiction. Characters and events in this novel are the product of the author's imagination. Any similarity to persons living or dead is purely coincidental.

Books By James Bonk

<u>Light of the Ark Series</u>

1. Light of the Ark

2. Shadows of the Ark

3. Light of the World

- Isaiah and the Sea of Darkness (standalone prequel)

<u>More Fiction</u>

- Christian's Look Back at Life

Stay up to date on new releases and email exclusive content: https://hello.james-bonk.com/signup/

To those in the messy middle, who pick up their cross daily.

———◄○►———

Then He said to *them* all, "If anyone desires to come after Me, let him deny himself, and take up his cross daily, and follow Me."
–Luke 9:23 NKJV

Contents

Chapter One

Hello, Christian

"Hello, Christian. Welcome."

"Please, call me Chris."

"Chris. It's nice to meet you. I know you didn't get a choice in picking your sponsor, and to be honest, we don't get to choose as well, but I've looked over your material and I expect us to do well together."

"I...I don't mean to be rude," Chris said as he fidgeted with his hands, "but I don't really need these extra sessions. Is there an assigned reading or something like that I can do? I don't want to waste your time, and I'm sure you can help plenty of others, the people who really need it."

"That's nice of you to think of others. But to answer your question, no, there is no further reading than what you have already seen. And I disagree with you; this is exactly what you need. It's why you're here, and it's why I'm here."

Chris looked away from Michael as his arms loosely crossed and his shoulders slouched forward.

"Please, have a seat." Michael motioned to the orange plastic chair that sat in the middle of the giant room with wooden floors. It was Chris's old high school gymnasium, where he could still remember first-period Personal Fitness class from nearly thirty years ago. It was also the same high school where Chris's son, Jake, was currently a senior.

Chris shuffled his feet, reluctantly kicking them forward with every step. He was forty-six years old but always felt like a small boy in these sessions, like they forced him to sit in the dentist's chair and endure painful drilling.

Michael was the second "sponsor" that Chris had met in the past five years at the modest mental health organization. They focused on helping those with rare mental disorders, and Chris had never heard of anyone in his condition prior to coming here.

Five years ago, Chris was in a horrible traffic accident involving multiple cars. A strange condition developed immediately afterwards in which he could remember every moment in his life before the accident. From the most mundane to the most extreme, all he had to do was close his eyes and think about it, and he'd instantly be there, reliving it for as long as he wished until deciding to return to the exact moment he closed his eyes. It was hardly longer than a blink in his current situation, but he could be gone for hours, days, months on end if so compelled.

At first, it felt like a superpower. He could walk by the grocery store and remember walking through it with his wife and son. He remembered the exact items, the exact price, and the exact time of day that Jake would help him put into the cart. But it was more than a photographic memory; he could remember his feelings, his thoughts, every single detail of the situation: the smell of the rotisserie chickens as he walked into the grocery store, the fresh and colorful berries in the produce section, the smooth surface of the wine bottle as he picked it up and balanced the weight, and all the times his wife squeezed his arm tight to stay close.

As he walked past structures in the small, overcast town, he relived joyful moments over and over. The Super Bowl party back in his twenties with his soon-to-be wife as they watched his favorite team close out the big win. They were dating exactly a month at the time and he remembered forgetting the game when she kissed him in celebration. It was his first memory of love for his wife. She cared nothing for football, yet was as emotionally invested in the game as he was, sitting on the edge of their seats during the plays and laughing off the tension during the highly anticipated commercials.

Other moments, such as golfing with his best friends. The joyful explosion when he sank the twenty-foot chip shot to save par for their group. The agony of landing three straight shots in the water as his friends ribbed his wild drives.

However, as time went on, he spent more time in his head, remembering related moments of the past and being less in the moment. Gradually, he grew distant from his family. Whatever happened, he had a corresponding memory to slip off into, returning in body but unable to communicate the emotions from the past.

His son was twelve at the time of the accident, and in the prior five years, they played catch or tag or whatever game of the season in their backyard countless times. However, in the five years since, zero. Chris couldn't even say "countless" anymore when he thought of playing with his boy. Given his mysterious condition, he went back and lived each moment. He knew that in the five years before his accident, he and Jake played in their backyard exactly nine hundred and thirteen times. He had the tallies on notepaper to prove it, averaging once every two days.

Chris would relive the first time his son learned to throw a spiral, the first time he gave the baseball enough power for Chris's palm to tingle in pain, or the first time he put a spin on the soccer ball and watched it bend in the air. That was one of Chris's proudest moments, watching his son figure out not only the strength but the finesse required to put the proper spin on the ball. But after years of missing playtime, Jake was more wrapped up in his team sports, his friends, his own life. Father-son time was gone.

The gap between Chris and his only child was not the only growing divide in the family. Chris and his wife, Evelyn, stopped communicating as well. Evelyn tried, Chris knew she was doing her best as night after night she would talk to herself as she willed Chris to care, to respond, to just be there. She would cry about how she missed him, for him to say something, say anything. But every time, Chris was speechless. He tried ...he really did. But every fight led him into a memory. He'd return and know it'd all be fine. It would be okay. Evelyn would understand, she'd come around. She always did.

When he moved out of the house, there was not a huge fight. No thrown dishes and curses. He didn't sit down with his son to tell him he still loved him, that he missed him and his mother. He never told Jake that it wasn't his fault, that sometimes things just don't work out. There was none of that. One day, Chris packed what he could carry and walked out of the house.

He didn't go far, renting an apartment just over a mile away, but the communication remained closed. Every time he looked at the phone, he thought of calling. But every time he thought of it, he didn't want to bother them; he would see them soon.

It would be okay...until it wasn't.

———————◆◦◆———————

After he moved out, Chris walked more than ever. Sunrise and sunset were his favorite times of the day. He liked to think it was the colorful skies and chilly temperatures that kept him out for hours at a time on most days, but deep down, he knew it was the lonesome apartment that he wanted to avoid.

He'd walk by the local coffee shops and pizzerias, by the ever-rotating corner stores that seemed to shift from fashion boutique to frozen yogurt to whatever new attempt at commerce that the season brought with it.

His most joyful, yet most painful, walk of each day was when he turned down the main road of his old neighborhood.

Most days, he wouldn't go into the subdivision, but every week or two, he mustered up the courage to stroll past the gates and walk down his old street. He was never sure if he wanted to see Evelyn or Jake. What would he say if they saw him? Nothing, he thought to himself. Nothing - PERIOD. He spent years not saying anything, so why should this time be any different?

Yet, his former home still drew him in as he remembered more of good times than the bad. The tickle fights with a five-year-old Jake. Picking up Evelyn and spinning her around when she hung up the call that announced her big promotion.

As much as he tried to stay in the wonderful moments, he could not avoid drifting into regrets. The time he broke the lock on Jake's door after the boy slammed the door in his face. He spanked the boy as hard as he could that night. The boy wasn't rebelling; he was just upset. Chris was upset himself, but Chris lost it and slapped his bottom so hard, his hand hurt.

The sad memories of Evelyn: fights over money, forgetting their fifth anniversary, all those weekends where he just *had* to go into work. He never cleared the air after a fight with Evelyn; they eventually came to an unspoken understanding and went to sleep, restarting the next day fresh.

The memory of Evelyn was the reason he first entered the facility and met his introductory sponsor. He tried to avoid that memory—it ate at him—but seeing his friends at a local restaurant/bar, *The Evening Lounge*, helped him deal with the memories. After Chris moved out from Evelyn and Jake, he went to the lounge nearly every night.

He sat with his old buddies, the other regulars, and talked remember-when, shoulda-coulda, and if-only all night long. It was easier to talk here when there was nothing in particular to discuss. Chris would have his typical soda water and his friends would have their drink of choice: some would drink pop, others beer, and a few others hard liquors. Every night was the same, even down to the place's owner, Praeda. The tall Italian with jet-black hair and the shoulders of a former bodybuilder. He gave the same old sarcastic greeting, ribbing them about nursing drinks and never ordering enough food for a real bill.

One night, as Chris finished his walk by approaching the lounge, a particular memory of Evelyn came to mind. It was one of the simplest memories of her that stuck with him and he relived it as he approached the bar. The brief memory, where Evelyn touched his cheek then gave him a soft kiss before resting her head on his shoulder, came into his mind, and he embraced it willingly as he walked. It stayed with his thoughts as he flashed back, not realizing that he didn't turn left to enter the lounge. Instead, he walked straight ahead and eventually landed in the group meeting in the high school gym.

Chris hated the first meeting. His sponsor, Clara, was nice enough, but one of those perfect ladies who was so happy, it made you sick. Clara ran the group meetings and would immediately pull Chris into the group discussion portion. He forced himself to show up at least once a month. Evelyn would appreciate that he was trying. Clara urged him to show up more often, to be more engaged in the community to see the benefits. But in Chris's point-of-view, showing up twice a week to hear how others talk about their feelings, the impact their conditions had on their family, and their renewal to embrace their situation as a gift? Ugh.

Chris tried not to be heartless but rolled his eyes in the dragged-out sessions every time someone made a quote-unquote *re-born breakthrough*, as Clara put it.

It shocked Chris to think it had been five years since his first visit; others had come and gone. They moved some that seemed to enjoy the sessions into other groups, and Chris lost track of them. Yet others who fidgeted and fussed the whole time gradually dropped out or moved into one-on-one sessions. Chris saw many of the dropouts at the lounge; they'd come and go, some angry and some sad with whatever troubles their conditions were causing, but all coming in to kill their time.

"So," Michael said as Chris sat in the surprisingly comfortable orange plastic chair, "What's on your mind?"

"Ummm," Chris stalled. He realized he was now one of those *types* moved from the group sessions into one-on-one coaching. He loved the idea of not having to listen to everyone else, but now he couldn't avoid the conversation. He couldn't hide his apathetic responses.

Michael waited patiently for Chris's answer as he smiled, not a huge grin but a welcoming soft smile that showed calmness and caring. The expression invited Chris into the conversation as the two locked eyes.

"Not to be rude," Chris broke eye contact, "but honestly, I wasn't thinking of anything."

"Yeah?" Michael questioned as his head dipped and he looked over his glasses at Chris.

"Yeah," Chris quickly responded.

Michael nodded in acceptance, comfortable in what Chris viewed as a terribly awkward silence.

Chris didn't admit it, but his actual thoughts were on how big Michael was. Praeda, who claimed to have won multiple European Strongman competitions in his younger days, was the most muscular person Chris knew. Michael did not have the obvious muscle definition of Praeda, but was at least 6'6" and solid as a rock, or maybe more like a small mountain. The glasses and but-ton-up shirt took away from Michael's dominating physique, which rested under neatly trimmed salt and pepper hair and two-day stubble.

Finally, Chris broke the silence with his curiosity. "Why did I get moved from the group? How does that work?"

Michael's warm smile grew as he eyed Chris before responding, "To help those along who don't seem to respond to the group sessions."

"So you think I need help?" Chris asked.

"Everyone needs help, Mr. Flagler." Michael gave an inaudible laugh. "However, our organization's choice is to work here with limited resources. The group sessions work for many, but certainly not all, so here we are."

"Yes, here we are," Chris trailed off as his eyes wandered around the room. He saw the old gym bleachers, pushed up against the walls. The halls leading to locker rooms and restrooms were dark. Only the emergency lights, which always remained on in certain parts of the gymnasium, shined bright over Michael and Chris.

Michael looked Chris over, studying him as Chris continued to avoid eye contact. Then Michael broke the silence with a firm voice. "Why did you show up?"

"What?" Chris questioned, taken aback by the direct question. Clara was never so direct in the group sessions. "What do you mean, why did I show up? I want help with my condition. That's what you do, so I'm here."

Michael nodded with his gentle smile. "No, you don't."

Chris was confused. "What?"

"No, you don't want help," Michael clarified.

"I'm here, aren't I?" Chris stated in a defensive tone.

"I do appreciate that. In the end, simply showing up is a major part of victory. But there is more, and you are hiding," Michael said without changing the tone in his voice.

"Look, I'm here. What are we going to cover today? Can we talk about my memories and how to live with them?"

"We won't be talking about living with them," Michael replied matter-of-factly.

Chris was getting upset at how plainly Michael spoke. "And this is what we're covering; I want you to tell me why you came here today."

"I came because..." Chris's frustration mounted. "I want help with my condition, I'm sick and tired of not being able to..." Chris spoke bolder, losing his passiveness. "To talk to my son; to be with my wife. I...I...I WANT TO LIVE AGAIN!"

Michael's light smile turned into more of a grin, and it only ignited Chris further.

Chris stood up. "WHAT'S SO FUNNY?"

"Oh, not funny. I'm happy."

"You're happy that my life is in shambles and I get NO resolution by coming here. Good. Glad you are happy." Chris sat back down, feeling bad for snapping at his new sponsor at their first meeting. *Great way to start off,* he thought to himself.

Michael remained silent.

"Look, I'm sorry," Chris relented. "I haven't burst out like that before. I just don't know how to live with this anymore."

Michael's smile never waned during Chris's outburst. However, it seemed to fuel it.

"I think that is enough for today. Thank you for coming in."

Chris spun his head, making eye contact again. "WHAT? We just started!"

"It's not about the time, Christian. It's about the impact."

"Call me Chris," Chris responded, putting his hand up in a stopping motion. "No one calls me that anymore. And how am I supposed to live with this if we only talk for a minute?"

Michael politely stood up as Chris finished speaking. "I suggest you enjoy it while you can. And we won't be talking about living with your condition. We're going to talk about moving on despite it."

Michael bowed his head as his tall frame towered over Chris. "Until next time, Mr.

Flagler." Then he strolled out of the dimly lit gym.

Chapter Two

Messy Middle

Chris walked through the outskirts of the overcast downtown area, getting back into the nearby suburbs that filled the pocket of land in between the downtown high rises and the nearby river that cuts through the west side of town.

It was a cold, gloomy night, and the sunset painted a canvas in pink and orange. The vibrant colors snuck their way through the thick sheet of dark gray clouds. Chris didn't notice the pleasant colors as he walked, head down, around the fountains and strip plazas toward his apartment. He didn't actively think about going to the lounge that night, but out of habit took the turn and entered, taking his seat near his small crowd of regulars.

As the night went on, he was quieter than normal. He thought about Michael's comments, how he said Chris didn't want help. "No, you don't." Michael's words rang in Chris's ear. For a moment, he wished he could relive it, like his life before the accident, but for whatever reason, he could only revisit events in his own life before the crash. His normal, same old memory was all he had of everything after the crash.

The lounge filled up quickly that night as happy hour bled into an early start on a late night. It quickly became a standing room only as couples, partiers, and many others piled in. They cramped the area around Chris and his friends.

Praeda looked busier than ever, but that was what made him tick. Chris stood up, opting to leave instead of wading through the sea of bodies to get another drink. He caught Praeda's eye and the delight on his face showed through the commotion.

The busy bartender motioned to Chris for another, but Chris waved him off and gave a point to the door. Praeda raised his hands, palms up, at his side and mouthed *WHAT* in disbelief that anyone would leave such a hot spot before it peaked.

As Chris tried to get through, the mass of people seemed to grow tighter, and a wave of them stood in between him and the exit, forming a wall of conversing friends.

He patiently slipped through one, then another, as the crowd mindlessly banged into him without consideration or notice until a violent shove pushed a young man directly into him, nearly knocking him over as he caught the guy. Chris thought the shoved person couldn't be much older than his son Jake.

As Chris helped the young man back up, the younger man struggled to find his footing. He was well beyond his drinking limit and stumbled back into Chris's arms. He tried to get the man back on his feet, but Chris felt like he was trying to balance a flagpole on its end. No matter the set point,

Chris prayed the young man balanced himself at the apex of his wavering.

The young man did not find balance and briskly stumbled back into whatever disagreement forcefully brought him into Chris's lap. Chris took the opportunity and stepped away, but the crowd was thick and he couldn't get far. He saw a path to the exit, but before he could get closer, an attacking howl of a scream came at him, preceding a thrown punch.

A group fight was breaking out, and Chris was in the middle of the commotion. He tried to dip his head and avoid the strike, but it came too quickly, glancing off the side of his head above his ear. He felt the watch of the person striking him cut across his scalp.

Chris shoved the offender back into the melee, where two brawlers turned into a group of four and resembled more a mosh pit than a social gathering. Before Chris could pivot away from the mess, another man put his shoulder into Chris and brought them both into the other four.

Fists swung and hands gripped tight as Chris tried to duck, but an elbow caught his back, near his spine. Turning to face the striker, a knee from the other side struck his leg, causing him to drop to one knee and hold his leg.

He was a mid-forties divorced father caught up in a bar fight with a group of twenty-some year olds, and he felt his frustration growing, just like it had when Michael challenged his reason for showing up.

He found a moment of solace as he held his leg, his adrenaline and frustration building. Balling his fist, he struck back at the body in front of him, catching a rib and feeling it crack. He bounced his shoulder off the next fighter, forcing him into the crowd and making space for Chris to take a few steps forward. Another strike, and then another. He pummeled the brawling bodies in front of him. Gradually, he was clearing the way.

Then a direct shot to his upper cheek near his temple hit him like a ton of bricks. He dropped to the ground as the lights in the lounge flashed, the music halted, and a booming scream from Praeda came through the crowd.

"HOLD!" Praeda screamed as he grabbed two of the culprits by the collar and effortlessly moved them aside like he was picking up a screaming toddler.

The owner of the lounge bent down and helped Chris up. "You alright?"

Feeling dazed, Chris shook his head. "Yeah, I'm good."

"Well, if that won't wake you up, nothing will." Praeda laughed. "Come on, next drink is on me." Praeda motioned Chris back toward his table.

Chris looked up and saw his table. The group stared back.

Waving a goodbye to them, Chris then motioned to Praeda. "No, I'm good, Praeda. I just want to get out of here for now."

Praeda looked confused, if not a bit hurt, by Chris leaving, but he eventually nodded back and helped Chris through the crowd and out of the lounge.

———◆○◆———

The next morning, Chris woke up to a throbbing eye and a sore body. All the fists, knees, and elbows left their marks deep in his tissue.

Looking in the mirror, locking eyes with himself and peering deep into his own eyes, he couldn't understand how he had gotten here. Twenty years ago, he was happily married with a great job. A dozen years ago, he was playing with his young son and talking about family vacation plans with his wife.

But now...he dropped his head as his arms extended in front of him, holding his drooping frame over the apartment's outdated and discolored bathroom sink. He shook his head as he forcefully shut his eyes, feeling the swelling from the blossoming black eye.

Looking back up at the mirror, seeing his own watery eyes, he asked himself, "How did you get here?"

Turning his back against the faded white tiles of his bathroom wall, he slid down to the floor and pulled his knees up to his chest, wrapping his arms around his legs. His forehead rested on his knees.

He missed his wife.

He missed his son.

He missed the life he left behind.

He sat alone on the bathroom floor and he cried.

———◆◇◆———

A large purple oval surrounded Chris's eye as he greeted Michael during their next session.

To Chris's surprise, Michael did not ask about the bruised eye but only spoke a soft, "Hmph," raising his eyebrows in a *well look at that* sort of way. The large sponsor extended his hand to greet Chris and welcome him back to the large, dimly lit gymnasium with two chairs in the middle.

Chris felt foolish. His body battered, he felt weak, and now he remembered the last meeting with Michael. The direct questions frustrated him. As soon as he sat down, he wished it was over, questioning himself for coming and doubting whether he would find any help here.

Michael sat down in front of him and began the session, breaking his racing thoughts. "What's on your mind?"

Taken aback by the open-ended question, Chris thought for a moment. It surprised him that Michael did not pick up where he left off, with a *why are you here* type question. Regardless, he still did not know how to answer the question.

Michael seemed perfectly content to wait for a response, the same warm smile across his face that somehow reminded Chris of a father watching a toddler attempt their first steps, but unsuccessfully falling back on their padded diaper. The large man sat in brown slacks and a light blue sweater, a change from the jeans and collared shirt, but still in a business casual, professional look.

After a moment of thought, and remembering his night of tears on the bathroom floor, Chris was honest. He was out of the group sessions, where it seemed he could never get an actual word in, and who knows how long he would even come back to these one-on-one talks. *Why not simply be honest and see how it goes?* He thought.

"What's on my mind..." he repeated as he opened up the floodgates of his real self for the first time. "Well...my eye, for one. I feel it pulsing and feel like everyone stares at me for a moment too long, like they are wondering what in the world happened. But even more than my eye, my back." He leaned over and awkwardly reached his arm around his back. "I'm not sure if it's my spine or my ribs back there, but something hurts like crazy and it wakes me up at night. I can't get comfortable."

"And what else?" Michael asked plainly.

Chris sat back in the plastic orange chair, shifting and wincing to get his injured back in the proper alignment. "I...I don't know." He looked down and to the side as he thought.

Michael remained quiet, noticing Chris was more in thought than avoidance.

"I mean, it's hard to deal with, ya know?"

Michael nodded, encouraging Chris to continue.

"It was so cool to see everything in my life at once, like I was in full control of not only the present but the past," Chris flashed a smile as he spoke, but it quickly subsided as he shook his head. It reminded him of all the times the past kept him from participating fully in the present. "But then, I just wasn't there. I was not there when my family needed me and I feel like...I feel..."

Michael again nodded as he leaned forward. His motion encouraged Chris to spit out the thought he was struggling to verbalize. "I feel worthless."

Silence filled the air as Chris returned Michael's eye contact. Michael tightened his mouth and turned his bobbing nod into a slow, wide-ranging *yes* motion. Chris thought for a moment that Michael would stand up and end the session, but for once, he did not want it to end. He felt good getting that off his chest.

"Tell me more," Michael responded.

"Okay." Chris thought before continuing. "I mean, I go for walks every day, but I never go talk to my wife or son. They probably don't want to see me, or even miss me. I spent my entire life trying to do what's right and then it all slipped through my fingers. And the worst part is," Chris was on a roll now, not deliberating each response but addressing them as they came, "the worst part is that I never even realized it. I never noticed my demise."

Chris abruptly stopped and looked at Michael, who seemed to take it all in.

"What's the real challenge for you here?" Michael eventually responded.

Chris frowned as he thought of his response, then lifted his head up to Michael. "I don't know what I'm doing. Why am I here? And not just here, with you, but in general. If God has some grand plan, yet my life is falling apart, I can't connect how in the world my failures help anything, help anyone. How is this a part of *HIS* plan?" Chris brought his hands up and joined them above his lap, grasping them tight and then releasing as he threw up his palms. "What's the point? I just feel so...so worthless."

Chris sagged his head as Michael remained quiet, taking in what he saw as a breakthrough.

Michael pivoted his questions and guided the conversation more directly. "You mentioned *God's Plan*. What makes you think there is a plan?"

"My parents brought me to church, but, I mean...we rarely go anymore. I think this world is more than randomness, more than some billion-year self-selection process that formed us. I don't know. Maybe that is just me being scared to admit that none of us know, so we grab on to whatever makes us feel good."

"I don't think admitting that you don't know is mutually exclusive to God having a plan. Those don't have to be separate things. I don't know what the city planner is doing to ensure our sewage system works properly, but I am delighted that the toilet works. I also know I can't flush cement mix down the drain and expect my plumbing to work properly."

Chris smiled for the first time that day. It was the most he had heard Michael speak, and he enjoyed hearing his sponsor's personality come out. "Are you comparing God's Plan to a city planner and humankind to a sewage system?"

Michael laughed in response. "I suppose I was, but in a good way." Michael's soft smile grew slightly. "I knew I would enjoy our sessions."

"Glad to hear it," Chris said sheepishly, but then cracked a smile again. "But I'm still envisioning your comparison. Why would anyone pour cement mix down their drains?"

"You'd be surprised what people do to themselves, and most don't even realize the harm they are causing."

Chris remained silent as he listened.

Michael continued, "No human is perfect, and if you're a Bible-believer, you know Jesus was as close as it gets, but he was *of God*, so I don't really count that as a perfect human. Knowing you are not perfect, and no one around you is perfect, can help you understand others and the crazy decisions they may make. But more importantly, it helps give yourself grace."

"Yeah, I suppose," Chris said, reluctantly agreeing.

"Think of it this way: set your mental condition to the side for a moment and think of all humanity on a line, a distribution of everyone where one end of the line is purely wicked and the other is purely good."

"Okay," Chris said as he saw a line in his head and mentally began seeing dots scatter across it.

"No one sits on the endpoints. Not one human is purely good or purely evil."

Chris nodded. "I can't argue with that, but—"

"But what is my point, you are thinking." Michael preempted Chris's train of thought. "My point is, if you understand that no human lies on the far side of the spectrum, whether good or evil, then you understand that everyone on this earth is in the messy middle. That everyone is striving to do what *they* think is right to move them along the line that *they* think they should go. If everyone is in the messy middle, then everyone has problems, everyone wants to get better, but take a step back to view it all. Ultimately, they all just bounce around in the middle."

"Okay, I can see that." Chris imagined a giant cloud of dots all climbing over each other trying to get to the *GOOD* side of the line, but as some dots moved closer, others naturally fell behind. The whole cloud of dots churned in his mind's eye.

"But if we can never get to where we want to go, what do we do?" Chris asked.

"That's not a simple answer. It's different for everyone."

"But where do we start?"

"Great question, Christian. First, you have to show up."

Chapter Three

Slums, Golden Roads, and the Unknown

"What's on your mind?" Michael asked to open up Chris's next session.

Chris took a moment and thoughtfully considered his response. "I don't know where we go from here."

"What do you mean?"

"Well, don't get me wrong. Our last meeting was the best I've had here. And I was actually looking forward to coming today, but..."

Michael gave his typical encouraging smile that Chris was growing accustomed to. He waited for Chris to continue.

"You know, when I left our last session, I walked around and enjoyed the sunset by the river."

"That's great."

"And as I went home, I stopped by the lounge. The way you described the messy middle, how nobody is perfect, yet everyone is trying to be better...But in the moment, who knows if they are helping or hurting all those around them? What one person thinks is helping may actually be the wrong thing to do. I feel like I have a powerful urge to figure that out, to know I'm doing the right thing."

"Okay," Michael encouraged as he motioned for Chris to continue.

"Well, I couldn't see that desire in the others. Most people there are just there, and that's okay with them. And that seems fine to me. To each his own..." Chris trailed off, unable to verbalize his thoughts concisely.

After a moment of pause, Michael interrupted Chris's thoughts. "What is the real challenge for you here?"

The question brought Chris's mind back to the conversation. "For me...I don't know, it's...Ever since our last meeting, I can't just enjoy the moment while at the lounge. But I feel crazy because no one else seems to feel that way. And now that I put some thought into it, I don't think anyone there has ever done a single thing differently. It's the same ol' thing, night in, night out." He sputtered a moment and then blurted it out. "Why am I different? Why...I mean, WHY to all of it?"

"Tell me more about that night at the lounge, when you started thinking and feeling this way."

Chris sat up straighter in his chair as he thought back. "There's another guy who goes there a lot too, Vic Fraus, a nice guy. He is about my age and has a couple of kids with his wife. Perfect family kind of thing. Their older boy is in Jake's grade. They're friends and play on some of the same teams. We run into each other a lot, especially after his office had a fire and he works from home now. We see each other nearly every night."

"Alright." Michael held his soft grin, encouraging Chris.

"So, I go into the lounge and start thinking about my condition. Trying to view it as a blessing in relation to how we are all in the messy middle we talked about, but I can't shake how everything has changed since the accident. You'd think it'd be for the best. I mean, I can remember everything down to the smallest detail, at any single point in my life leading up to the accident, yet I do not know what to do with it. Every night I wish I was sleeping next to my wife. I go back in my mind and remember how she crossed one leg over mine so we could touch. I go walking and come home wishing I could ask Jake about his day, find out how his classes are coming, how practice was, thoughts on college. But no. It's just me. Me and my thoughts, my memories. Nothing is real anymore, and..." Chris shook his head as his eyes watered. "I'm just flat out UNHAPPY and don't know what to do about it."

Michael looked on intently as Chris continued. "Meanwhile, as I'm thinking this, Vic strolls in. He has a great job, a wonderful house, a beautiful wife who volunteers and organizes everything you can imagine, and his beautiful kids always seem to be on the Honor Roll and best players on their teams."

"Are you talking about how your experiences can be so different?" Michael questioned.

"Yes...but no, see, that's not it. I used to think that, questioning why he had it so great. Why couldn't we be like that? We are really no different. He's just like me. I saw it in his eyes the other night when he stopped by the lounge and we talked a bit. Our boys are both playing lacrosse this spring and we talked about the coach and the conditioning program he's got all the kids doing in the off-season. And as we talked, I could see something in his eyes I never noticed before. He was sad. On the surface, his body language said he was having a blast. He is the life of the party nearly every night. But his eyes told a different story. I don't think he'd ever admit it, but I saw it, plain as day. He was sad, just miserable. And ultimately, that puts him in the same boat as me."

Michael eyed Chris attentively as Chris continued. "So...what I'm getting at is, if I'm striving for all that Vic has, but he's still just as miserable as me, then I don't know where we go from here. All I want is my family back, my old life, but Vic has all that. He even knows my story, we've talked about it, so I don't think he's ungrateful for what he has or putting up some incredible façade. But if Vic can't be happy with all that, then I don't know if I could ever be happy. And if that is true, then I'm stuck like this," Chris looked down at himself and back up at Michael. "This is me...forever."

"I see," Michael commented as he paused and thought. "That is hard to deal with."

They sat in silence for a moment. Chris began feeling helpless as he stepped his way back through all the reasoning he just laid out.

A moment later, Michael restarted the conversation. "Let's back up. You mentioned a thought: 'Why am I different?' as you thought of Vic. Tell me more."

"Yeah. I mean, even if he is just as miserable as me, at least he gets to be with his family. He doesn't have to live in a crappy apartment and question himself every second of the day, but in the end, what's the point? Why try to be happy in this world?"

"There are some who think this place is more of a waiting room, a temporary home, until you get to the ultimate place that contains unimaginable joy," Michael responded.

"Heaven?" Chris asked. "Yeah, I was religious as a kid, but...Ya know, it falls away."

"Did it fall away, or did *you* fall away?" Michael asked directly.

"It doesn't fit my work schedule, and I mean all the research I have to do on global markets, especially developing markets...it's hard to see God when you see the slums of the world. All those horrible places and how some people live."

"Interesting. I think that would help you *see* God, not dismiss him."

"Why? Seeing children in their own filth. Beggars, thieves, and orphans all roam the streets alike while corruption runs rampant through their patchwork government. I think that reflects more Hell than Heaven."

"Are you comfortable with the idea of Heaven and Hell?" Michael questioned.

"Of course, I know the high-level stuff, and we went to church regularly years ago, but then only for holidays. Eventually, it stopped. I mean, we'd try to see family on holidays, so it just...sort of fell off."

"What would this world be if it did not have those slums you referred to?" Michael asked.

Chris thought for a moment, imagining only pristine cities in between gorgeous rolling fields of the countryside, and then he gave a slight laugh. "Probably close to what I always imagined what Heaven looked like as a kid, shining golden roads."

"Exactly," Michael responded. "And what about the opposite, if the world was only those slums?"

Chris raised his eyebrows to Michael, his body language asking if that was a real question. "Then the pendulum swings to its opposite end. That'd be total Hell on Earth."

"So your world is somewhere in between Heaven and Hell?" Michael posited.

"Yes, and I suppose...I suppose that makes sense," Chris responded.

"Mind if I tell you my opinion?" Michael asked.

"Please." Chris leaned forward, realizing Michael rarely offered his own opinion over asking Chris a question.

"I think the slum of this world is a case *for* God."

"How so?" Chris sat back in his chair, a skeptical look covering his face.

"If you read the material, the Bible, I mean, then you know God made this world. God is perfect, he proclaims what he made is *good*, but sin happens in the garden and now *His* perfect world, the garden built for man, is no longer perfect. Immediately, the world is a rough, unforgiven world where sin is now a part of mankind's core fabric."

"Yes. That sounds awful," Chris said plainly.

"Yet, in a world filled with sin, a world that struggles to stay apart from God. How come the Bible talks about loving your neighbor as yourself? How come Jesus died for you?" Michael asked rhetorically. "If there is no hope in the slum, then where do the greatest acts of love, of life, come from?"

Chris sat silently as he listened.

Michael continued, "Furthermore, if God *is* perfect and he is in control, then how could something corrupt what a perfect being made? That would mean he either lost control or is *not* perfect. But by definition would imply that He is not perfect to begin with."

Chris thought as Michael continued.

"You said the slum makes you think of Hell. It makes me think of Heaven. The beggar, the thief, the orphan; they all are products of sin in your world and may or may not have put themselves in their own situation. But regardless of their situation, of where they sit in the messy middle of everyone, of all the sinners, there is hope. An orphan child may grow up and embrace sin, only perpetuating the horrible side of life, or she could find the love of life hidden in the muck. The child could grow up to show others kindness and love, rebuking evil. And if only one person in your world, of all the billions that have lived and yet to come, embraces the love amid all sin, then doesn't that show there is a pure love somewhere out there? Hidden in the messy middle? And that love, that perfectness that shines in the darkness, has to have a source. It has to come from somewhere."

Chris looked at Michael, not knowing how to respond. He thought to himself, *Yes, of course!* But something held him back. Michael's simple argument of seeing the beauty within the ugly, the idea of good rising from the muck of sin spoke to Chris. Yet he could not verbalize the hint of the warm feeling he felt deep inside. The feeling was so odd to him. It felt new, and he questioned it.

He looked at Michael and could see an expression of hope on his sponsor's face.

Hope.

Michael's expression matched the sliver of hope that beat deep inside Chris's core.

A smile gradually broke across Chris's face as he embraced the feeling of hope; that things could get better.

But to his dismay, only a breath later did his mind wander past the sense of hope from Michael's discussion and into the inevitable. Despair and hope, sin and redemption, all of it led to one place. Chris could see his whole life behind him, at any moment he wished, but his special condition did not apply to his existence after the accident. He could not go back and relive his sessions with Michael, never again see last night's sunset, and never go back to speak up during the times he wished he said more to Evelyn or to Jake. Chris's hope made him realize the finite time he had, and that he was wasting it.

The feeling of hope abruptly left his chest, like rushing water down the drain. An empty feeling filled the void, as if someone had punched him in the stomach and lost the air in his lungs.

As the void inside him filled his heart and mind, he suddenly felt as if *something* wanted him, something longed for his existence. And all he had to do to cooperate was ignore the hope. Just be complacent with his current self.

Don't go toward hope. Don't think that. It's not for you.

He felt himself pulled toward the thoughts of the void, as if it planted the thought in his mind and it was taking root. It whispered to him as his thoughts aligned with the void's message, ignore the hope and live forever. He could always relive the good times with Evelyn, with Jake. Every night, he could go to the lounge and reminisce. His mind could stay in the past while his body ignored the unknown, the risk of what was to come.

The unknown. The empty void in his chest filled with fear.

Chris thought of the lounge, where he could sit in peace, remembering the better days. Where he could slip in and out of his past and be with others. Where no one ever talked about the next steps, but they embraced the unknown void. It was easier there.

Chris stood up. With a polite smile, yet not making eye contact, he nodded at Michael and walked toward the exit.

Before he was out of sight, he turned to see his sponsor.

The look of hope, unchanged, on Michael's face, looked straight back at Chris.

Chapter Four

Regret

"What's on your mind?" Michael smiled at Chris in the dimly lit gymnasium.

"Sorry for leaving so abruptly yesterday," Chris responded.

"Want to talk about why you left?" Michael asked.

"It's hard to explain...I was feeling good as we talked, and you still have me thinking about the slums versus cities of gold, but I don't know...I don't know what's next for me. I don't know if I can give up what I have."

"A couple of sessions ago, you spoke about moving on, about how your life was not what you wanted it to be. Now you are feeling the opposite?" Michael spoke plainly, quickly recapping the prior conversations.

"I know, I know...It's just..." Chris looked around the room, avoiding Michael's direct eye contact. "It's hard. If I lose what I have, I won't be able to go back, to see them in my head anymore."

"You are unique, Christian, but I have seen this in other patients."

"You have?" Chris replied.

"Yes." Michael nodded. "Everyone has a fear over what they are leaving behind and for what's coming next, the unknown."

The word *unknown* struck Chris. It was the name he told himself over the empty feeling, the opposite of hope, the anti-hope as he thought of it when he left the prior session. He named it *The Unknown* in his mind, and Michael spoke as if he knew it was there all along.

"But before we talk about what we leave behind, let's talk about what's it for, moving forward and how the big events you had in your life each helped you move forward," Michael said.

"Like what?" Chris asked.

"For starters, did you debate or fear marrying Evelyn?"

"Nope." Chris reacted quickly. "Easiest decision I've ever made."

"And how about when you had Jacob?"

"No, it simply felt like the right time. I mean, we talked about it, of course, but there wasn't much debate. We agreed."

"Do you think you were the same person before you married Evelyn, or did you change after married life?"

Chris smiled, remembering the ways she forced him to keep the bathroom clean or the dress clothes she bought him. Over time, he adopted the cleaning and dress habits as his own. He unexpectedly came to love them without ever thinking about adopting them.

"No, I certainly changed over the years."

"And were you the same person after becoming a father?" Michael asked.

"No way." Chris's mind shot back to the late-night feedings when Evelyn set up a bottle for him so she could get a few hours of sleep. Then it shot to a memory of using a bad word in front of toddler-age Jake and hearing the young boy run in circles repeating it. He never used that word again. "No, I certainly changed after that too," Chris said with a half-smile.

"All those moments, you did not know what was in front of you. The unknown was there too, but you did not debate it; you accepted it and molded yourself for the better. For example, before marriage and a child, what would you have done with that bonus money you received a few years before your accident?"

Chris remembered this decision well. He expected the annual bonus, but he did not expect it to be so much, four times higher than normal because of an exceptional year. Meanwhile, his old truck needed more and more repairs. With every repair, he'd eye the new four-wheel model with a lift kit. That thing looked like it could climb a tree, and now he could buy it with cash. However, Evelyn had mentioned private school. Jake's classes seemed very crowded, and the teachers stretched thinner than ever.

They saw Jake struggling, and he needed a change, but the cost was high. Even on a dual income, they hadn't budgeted for such an enormous expense. They'd need to save up and wait another year before Jake could begin. However, Chris's bonus would get three, maybe four, years of private school paid for. Ultimately, the decision was straightforward, but whenever Chris saw that truck on the road, he felt like someone else had driven his truck off the lot.

Seeing the response in Chris's eyes, Michael gave a moment of pause, and then continued, "Even going back to when you were a kid, you were terrified of high school. You remember that?"

Chris nodded yes.

"Then going into college. Then all those awkward dates once you were a single professional before you met Evelyn. Every single moment shaped you and made you who you are." Michael paused again, letting the silence fill the air, as Chris took in the point.

Michael continued softly, "And it's more than just our bodies or our feelings at the moment. It's in your soul. Pain is for the flesh, while love and hope are for the soul. Tell me one more thing: I'd like to know if your accident was painful."

Chris's face went pale.

His accident...When his whole life changed. When he grew distant from his family. When his mental gift of remembering every exact detail before that time came into being. The gift he now thought of as more of a curse.

"My accident?" Chris said as he stalled.

"Yes. Please, describe to me what *physical* pain you remember."

"It all happened so fast." Chris used his gift as he pictured the event in his mind. He instantly flashed into himself in that exact moment, reliving the experience down to the detail, but quickly pulled himself back.

"I was driving my truck, heading to softball. I didn't even play anymore, not regularly, but was filling in for a friend in the church league just north of here...I don't want to do this. No, I don't want to see it, to see *them* again," he said plainly.

"I think it'll help, please. Relive it. Tell me what you see, hear, and feel this time around," Michael responded.

Chris was wary; he'd never relived this moment of his past. The horrible moment, such carnage, and even though it was an accident, was his fault. He didn't want to notice the other people, the cars next to him, the kids in their car seats playing with their toys and singing a song.

As he thought, he went back, driving his fifteen-year-old mid-sized black pick-up down the interstate. His custom playlist, made years ago, blared from his phone through a headphone jack wire connected to the car's radio. The pump-up and feel good mix of Christian rock and hip hop played on.

Chris took in the situation, exploring and observing like a guest in his own body. The body in his memory that went through the motions, the exact specifics, but the mind was of a different Chris. The different Chris, who sat in the cheap plastic orange chair across from Michael.

The truck sped along and banked a two-lane exit as one interstate flowed into another, going from west to northbound. He was fifteen minutes from the softball fields.

Chris waited to merge from the new lane that would soon be exit only. His truck quickly came up behind a brown sedan driving under the speed limit, never breaking fifty. Chris tried to stay patient. His body in the dimly lit gymnasium, sitting across from Michael, could feel the impatience pulsing through his past self.

Trying to avoid tailgating the sedan, he continued singing along to the music as he bobbed his head.

The cars piled up behind him in the two merging lanes, multiple cars eager to get over now to avoid the forced exit as regular traffic zoomed by at seventy in the left-hand lanes. Chris tried to get over, but the car behind him punched the gas and raced into traffic. He tapped his brakes and swerved back behind the slow-moving sedan to avoid being clipped by the passing car.

A family to his right also swerved in response. Chris could see the parents in the white four-door looking over to him, frustrated by the shift back and slow down. They were just as eager to get over and he was blocking their merge.

Two twin toddlers in the backseat, unaware of the mounting traffic, played with toys in their car seats. Their mouths moved along to a song unheard by Chris.

A semi now raced past on Chris's left. Through his mirror, he could see a gap behind the large carrier. As it passed, he gunned it. The old pickup jolted forward and kept pace with the backend of the large trailer as he sped up.

His impatience subsiding, he took a quick glance back to his right-hand blind spot and saw the family merging over safely as well. The person in the brown sedan holding up traffic was getting off, happily taking the forced exit and nonchalantly slowing down, not noticing the backup to their rear.

Turning his head back to the road, Chris noticed his softball mitt and cleats in the passenger seat, about to fall to the ground. He reached to push them back up fully on the seat as he turned the wheel gently to the left. Now out of trouble, he'd cruise past the semi in front of him and be on his way. He would have time to get a good warmup in before this game.

Chris's body in the orange plastic chair trembled as it observed what was about to happen. He knew what came next.

As he moved the wheel left, he never checked his driver-side blind spot. If he did, he would have seen a wall of a truck careening down the highway, well over the normal speed of traffic. As Chris's truck crossed the dotted line, the truck smashed into the back passenger door, right behind Chris and in front of the gas tank, spinning Chris sideways in an instant.

It all happened so fast.

He pulled himself out, back to face Michael, but then returned to crash, forcing himself to stay in the moment. To look, to hear, to see as Michael guided him to do. Michael was asking about the physical pain, but he only felt a quick flash of it as the semi trampled the pickup. Then it was over. He felt nothing.

He vaguely remembered the trailer of the semi swinging into the side of the family behind him, swiping the family off the road like a batted fly. He vaguely remembered the smell of burnt rubber as tires locked up. All those senses and fuzzy memories were a part of the quick flash of extreme pain, and then...nothing.

He remembered the pain as much worse than it really was. Michael was right, it was over quickly, but it was what Chris remembered next that drove his avoidance. Waking up in the hospital, the core fear of this memory was right in front of him.

The father from the white sedan. The family of four.

He couldn't remember the exact feelings in this moment the same as before his accident, but there were glimpses. Like a faded photograph, he could squint and make it out with dedicated focus.

After waking up in the hospital, Chris found himself in the hallway outside of his room. Endless beeps and alarms of the emergency room filled his ears.

The father walked out of a room in front of Chris. He sidestepped from the doorway and fell back to the wall. Looking up at the lights, Chris could see the man's eyes watering. He was fighting the urge to cry.

In a moment, the man quit fighting it. His chin dropped to his chest as his back slid down the wall. He sat on the floor, knees curled up to his chest as he buried his head in his hands.

The man cried uncontrollably. The muffled sobs rang in Chris's ears.

Chris remembered every detail of his life before the accident but hardly much of anything after the accident, but that cry...he would never forget that cry.

His complacency, his lack of awareness, caused it.

Back in their orange plastic chairs, Chris and Michael sat in silence as Chris reflected on the man. He was a husband, a father.

Chris had watched the man silently, and from that day on, the communication struggles with his family began.

As Michael waited patiently for Chris, the flash of pain Chris experienced in his truck, the last moment he remembered before waking up in the hospital, replayed in Chris's mind. It was the last memory he could replay. The quick, brilliant flash of pain was gone as soon as it arrived. It stuck in his mind. He replayed it repeatedly. He had never gone back to that moment, the accident, the pain, and then seeing the crying father in the hospital hallway and he stood in silence. Now he relived those minutes and hours again and again during the seconds that Michael waited.

"Now tell me about it: what you saw, what you heard, what you felt," Michael injected, pulling Chris from his memory.

"The music, the urge to move lanes, and then...It felt like my whole body was crushed, like it stabbed me all over my body, but that pain was over quickly." Chris paused and looked up at the ceiling as he continued, "But seeing the man from the other car in the hospital hallway that hurts more, a lot more. I caused that. He lost everything...because of me." Chris sniffed and opened his now-watering eyes wide, holding back the tears.

"The pain to your body is temporary, but the pain to your soul lasts far longer," Michael replied. "An event like that, it's horrible. Sometimes those moments are quick, and sometimes drawn out. Sometimes they are painful and sometimes it is but a mere flash, like in your case. But all of them, every single one, impacts your soul far more than your body. They are also more than pain; they are a chance to move on, to leave the old you behind."

"I was happy before my condition," Chris said, frustration in his voice. "Why, why me?

Why do I have to deal with this condition? I can't even live my life anymore."

"I cannot answer that," Michael responded bluntly to the rhetorical question. "By now, I think you are smart enough to realize that each of us can't know everything, if you'll admit it. We can't look upon the universe and be able to comprehend the design and purpose. But we can enjoy it, we can praise it, and we can fight back against the evils in the world that prevent us from loving are gifts and the people in our care."

"You know I disagreed with them," Chris shook his head as he pivoted the conversation, "and nearly got thrown out instead of walking out on my own."

Michael looked at Chris, encouraging him to elaborate.

"After our last session, when we talked about sadness and how I saw it in Vic, I was sitting in the lounge and I could see it in everyone. And the regret over wasting my life, I could see it in all of them too. No one there is happy, no matter how much they try. No...Not at that place."

Michael gave a slight smile as he listened. "Once you see, you cannot unsee."

Chris continued, "And I couldn't, just could not, sit there and rehash old stories anymore. It didn't feel right. I had to get out of there."

"And what happened when you tried to leave?" Michael asked.

"I didn't even have the chance to get up before Praeda brought us our next round, like he read my mind. And once he was at the table, he called me out. He asked why did I look like I was going to leave right after getting there, why I thought I was better than everyone else after he's helped me out so many times. It was like he knew I felt different, and it ticked him off. And then Vic picked right up on Praeda's frustration and told me to find a new table."

"What else?"

"I got up, but not without another comment from Praeda. I mean, he is usually sarcastic and gives everyone a hard time, but in a welcoming way, but this time, he seemed...pissed. He said, 'Don't think it's up to you, it's all random, it's a lottery, you're wasting your time.'"

Michael nodded, taking in the comment. "What else?"

"Nothing else. I just left and haven't been back since." Chris turned his head toward the ground and tightened his face as if trying to think through a complicated proof. "But now that we talk about it, maybe Praeda is right, that guy driving next to me, he lost his family and it was my fault, MY FAULT, not his. He had no idea that one moment he'd be cruising along, on to whatever family event they were going to or coming from, and then BAM, the worst possible thing he could imagine. It happens to him, to them. And he had NO awareness, NO control. Then me, I had NO awareness, NO control of that dang semi, speeding like a madman, that wiped me out. How is that fair? What's the point if ultimately we have no, and I mean ZERO, control over a situation like that?"

Chris stood up and turned away from Michael. "We are sitting ducks in this world, just waiting to either win the wonderful life lottery or get smacked by a Mack truck."

Chapter Five

Control

"It feels like such a waste," Chris said sadly, his frustration growing to acceptance as he sat back in his orange plastic chair.

"What does?" Michael asked.

"I mean all of it, the last five years, and honestly, Praeda isn't wrong. This is a lottery; we don't control our success."

"I certainly don't agree with that."

"Why don't you? WHY?" Chris's volume rose with his frustration, "Everything is going well, then WHAM! Accident happens, everything changes, and NOT for the better. My marriage tumbles, my relationship with my son breaks apart...." Chris quit talking as he shook his head and clenched his jaw.

"What *do* you control?" Michael asked plainly.

"What?" Chris turned back to his sponsor, incredulous at the simple dismissal of his frustration.

"Does the orphan child born into poverty choose her parents? Does the trust fund baby choose their inheritance? Or can someone choose to get cancer or choose to fall in love?"

"NO," Chris said sternly, holding tight to his frustration as he sat back down.

"What do all those people have in common?"

"Something horrible, or wonderful, happened to them. Outside of their control."

"That's right," Michael nodded, "and what does that prove about that person?"

"That they're lucky, or very unlucky," Chris said passively

"No," Michael retorted bluntly. Chris raised his attention and made eye contact with his sponsor.

Michael continued, "The outcome of a situation that is thrust upon a person tells us nearly nothing about that person. You can't choose your parents. You can't choose cancer. But you can do your best, and I mean YOUR, *you* as an individual, with *your choices*. You cannot choose how you start this life, or many things along the way, but you can do your best no matter the situation."

"Best," Chris said dismissively. "I tried my best. I was a good father, I was a good husband, and then out of nowhere, the universe sends me under a semi and gives me this condition. And I'm torn apart from my family. What does doing your best have to do with anything in the end?"

Chris bowed his head and drooped his shoulders, looking like a man accepting defeat.

"Praeda really did a number on you, huh?" Michael said.

Chris remained silent, wondering if he'd ever return for another session. He thought that he really was enjoying it before this conversation.

"You know, we were once close. Praeda and I," Michael said, interrupting Chris from his depressed thoughts.

Chris picked up his head. "That's hard for me to see. You two are polar opposites, well, outside of you both being huge, but your personalities..."

"It may seem that way now, but it wasn't back in the beginning. However small, even a slight change, compounded over time, can lead to a tremendous gap. But yes, years ago, when this place was still in its infancy, we were very close, best friends. We were going to take on all the challenges that mankind offered. We were on a mission."

"So what happened?"

"The *fullness* of life." Michael raised his eyebrows, giving a grandiose sense to the phrase.

Chris leaned forward as Michael continued, "Christian, life isn't all rainbows and sunshine. We each get dealt different cards, and we can perceive any individual situation as horrendous or absolutely terrific compared to another. It's all relative, and it's all about what you do with it. Just like you, Praeda didn't like the idea of external factors having such a big impact on people's lives. He wanted more awareness, more knowledge, of everything going on. He wanted control."

"So what happened?"

"Ultimately, he left us and went off to do his own thing. It caused quite a stir in our organization, and unfortunately, he has been trying to undermine us ever since. Listen to his words carefully and you'll hear it. Not that he hates the randomness in the world, it's that he hates not controlling it. He doesn't want *you* to choose, for you to do better with the cards this world deals you. No, he wants to choose for you."

"I don't get it," Chris replied. "If you don't take control of your life, then you'll get walked all over, but you're saying to accept what the universe, or whatever is *out there*, gives you."

"First off, you grew up religious, so you know what is *'out there.'* This isn't mysticism; we are a Christian organization. And there is a fine line between being a man or woman of action and accepting defeat. So, I'll ask you again, what do you control?"

"My choices," Chris shrugged, "but it doesn't sit right with me. You say 'religious,' which is okay, yeah, but even with that, then you have to deal with: 'if you believe in Christ, then you're forgiven and saved.' It's 'God saves you'; you don't save yourself. So what can I do? What's the point? Do my actions matter or don't they? Saul put Jesus's apostles to death and then flip a few pages, and Jesus is using him to spread the gospel across the entire region. A murderer, misaligned to what Jesus preached, gets saved, so when is Jesus going to knock me off my horse and help the scales fall off my eyes? Because it sure feels like I'm not in control, it doesn't matter, I'm just...waiting for...WH ATEVER. Just make it easy and knock me off the horse. Show me the light!"

Chris threw up his hands and leaned back in his chair before settling and looking back at Michael.

"Maybe I am here to knock you off your horse?" Michael questioned.

Chris looked at Michael curiously, while Michael sat unmoving, looking at Chris, with the same smile he always wore.

"Have you ever read Marcus Aurelius's 'Meditations'?" Michael asked.

"The Roman Emperor...from centuries ago? No."

"You should. It is sort of his diary, a combination of multiple notebooks that he wrote during his reign. It surprises some at how....how human they are, at how much a common man in today's time can identify with the struggles that he dealt with daily. And how he handled his thoughts about them."

"Yeah, must have been tough having all the money and all the power in the world," Chris said sarcastically.

"Did you ever get frustrated by coworkers?" Michael asked.

Chris nodded.

"So did he. Did you ever wonder what was your place in this world?"

Chris again shook his head yes.

"So did he. Have you ever thought about what will the world think of you when you are long gone? Of the impact of all your daily struggles and how many people spent their lives working toward something, only to be completely forgotten, lost to history in a mere generation or two. How your impact on this world is not even a pin-prick on all the years past and yet to come?"

"Well, not exactly like that, but...yes. Just like we were talking, 'what's the point?'"

"The same hopes and fears that you have today, he had two thousand years ago, as he was running the largest empire in the world. And do you know how he handled all those thoughts, the ones that could have sunk his confidence at a moment's notice?"

Chris listened silently.

"He dealt with them. He read, studied, and wrote on topics worthy of his thoughts. The Roman emperor realized you can influence the way you think. You can change that soundtrack in your head. It would have been nice to get him to take Jesus's teaching more seriously, but all things in due time." Michael flashed a sly grin. "My point is, he balanced the influences and impacts of the world on his life with his own free will. To apply his own principles so he could deal with the horrors of his world." Michael leaned forward, locking eyes with Chris. "You have no chance of controlling the world yourself. You can only do your best to control yourself and hope to influence your small piece of the world. If enough people do that, you can change the entire world."

Chris felt goosebumps swiftly cover his arms and a tingle shot up his back and over his scalp.

Michael continued, "Christian, you are right. There are horrible things in your world and you cannot choose where and how you start or whether a speeding semi shows mercy as it runs you over. But you can do your best, *YOUR* best, not anyone else's. It is your choice whether to sink into the muck of the world or to keep kicking long enough that your head remains above water."

Silence once again filled the large room as Chris thought.

"What happens when you sink?" Chris soon asked.

"You might not see the hand reaching down to pull you out," Michael replied. A moment of silence passed as Chris thought about what Michael had said, then Michael stood up. "Next time we meet, I'd like to know what *you* want. Five years ago, you had a painful ending to how you saw your world. Maybe it's time you had a joyful beginning."

Chapter Six

Admission

Chris left the session with Michael and took his normal long walk home, but this time, he did not enter the lounge. He crossed the street and walked past, watching the quiet entrance as it loomed and waited to welcome the dinner and nightlife crowd that would soon fill its walls. He continued on toward his old neighborhood.

He forced himself to think about Michael's question. What did he want? Being honest with himself, he had absolutely no idea. The usual things went through his mind: A good job with competitive pay, a loving wife and a well-behaved kid, a nice house, a family vacation once or twice a year, and it'd be nice to have a boatload of money in the bank.

He stopped himself, realizing he was playing in his mind what he thought the perfect life looked like for someone his age, in his situation. Of course, he wanted a loving family, a good job that paid well. All those things were security, safety. He had all those things, more or less, before his accident. So why was he still longing for something? Why did he still feel a hole in his chest?

As he zig-zagged through the rows of streets in his old neighborhood, he continued to think and look around at all the houses. Before long, he found himself in front of his old house, wondering if Evelyn or Jake were home. This time in the evening, he should be at practice or doing schoolwork. If they were home, Evelyn was likely cleaning up dinner.

He looked at his house. The black edges of the painted trim around the windows were fading. He remembered the crisp lines when the black trim was still fresh, the contrast they made against the light blue coloring that covered the outside walls. The yard looked wonderful; Evelyn must have finally hired a company. He remembered the weekends he fretted on the overgrown grass as he drove Jake to his lacrosse game early Saturday morning. Evelyn always wanted a lawn service to free up time, but not Chris. He complained about it being such a chore, but deep down, he loved it. The sense of accomplishment that came from a fresh-cut lawn.

Flashing back in his mind, he relived the first time he cut the lawn with his new mower. He took in the smell as he looked over the finished yard. It was like a green carpet. He smiled as he piled up clippings of the overgrown bush before brushing off the dirt covering his forearms and shins.

Michael asked him, "What do you want?" This was it. He wanted a purpose, he wanted to accomplish a task and then go inside to kiss his wife. To chat with her while he enjoyed a cold can of soda water that waited for him in the thirty-five-degree refrigerator. He wanted to see his son overcome the challenge of a different school assignment. To point the boy in the right direction and then watch that frustration slowly turn to progress, and then to accomplishment.

What did he want? He wanted to be there for his family, to guide them, to love them, to have a purpose.

A passing car interrupted his thoughts, the bright lights shining in his eyes. He wondered what he would say to Evelyn as she pulled into the driveway, thinking it must be her and Jake coming home.

His heart raced.

But uneventfully, the car passed by and the road returned to a calm silence.

He stood in the silence, turning back to his old house. What did he want? He wanted to do the right thing for his family.

Looping back around the neighborhood, through town, he walked and thought as the sun set on the sleepy town. The rays of the setting sun were finding their way through the overcast clouds and gray skies to give a brilliant purple and pink canvas stretched across the horizon.

Chris passed by the shops and restaurants, finding himself approaching the lounge. Once again, he crossed the street, but this time, the entrance was not sleepy; it was busy. The dinner crowd was leaving as the barflies and party-goers started packing in.

He laughed in his head about how many nights he spent there over the past five years, never giving it a second thought. Now, he could not avoid seeing the sadness, loneliness, and anger in the crowd as they forced smiles and conversation. He didn't want that anymore. Not for himself. He wouldn't wish it on anyone he loved.

Pulling his gaze away from the crowd, he turned to walk down the street, but something caught his eye as he looked away. He paused. "NO," he said aloud to himself, turning around and stepping over the curb on his side on the road to get a closer look.

It was Jake, walking into the lounge with a small group of friends.

Chris jogged over to the entrance of the lounge, calling out to his son, "Jake! Jake!" but received no response as Jake shuffled in and continued chatting with his friends. As Chris approached the entrance, two large men he recognized as other regulars came out and set up bar stools.

"Hold up," one man said abruptly as he held up his hand.

"Hey, guys, I come in here all the time. My son–" But the other man cut Chris off.

"Yeah, yeah, everyone knows someone, but let's see some ID, pal," the second man replied rudely as the first reached around the front door and pulled out a thin high-top table and placed a locked box on it.

"I'm twice the drinking age, fellas, and I've seen you guys here for months. Come on, my kid just went in."

"Maybe this isn't about age; maybe you're not a good fit for us anymore."

"What?" Chris questioned.

As Chris's confusion grew, Vic came out the front door and started talking to the wanna-be bouncers.

"Hey, Vic, Jake just went in and these guys are holding me up."

Vic looked up at Chris and faked a surprised expression. "Oh yeah? Hey there, Chris." Motioning back to the entrance, he said, "I know. He's with my boy, Louis, and some friends. Don't worry, I'll keep an eye on 'em."

"I just want to talk with him." Chris stepped forward, but the large arm of one bouncer raised up to his chest, holding him back.

"Nope," the man said sternly.

Chris turned his surprised expression toward Vic. "I just want to talk with him. Since when is this place a private party?"

Vic nodded his head toward the bouncer as the big man lowered his arm and he stepped close to Chris. "You know? I don't think Jake wants to talk to you anymore. From what I hear, you've been gone a long time, and it's time he moved on. It's time he became his own man."

"What does that have anything to do with me coming—" Vic cut him off as he moved in closer, getting right in Chris's face.

"I'm surprised you even want to come in. The last time you were here, you left as soon as you got here, and you sure ticked off Praeda, that's a fact."

"Vic, I've been going through some things, and now I—"

"Yeah, yeah, we all know you've been going to your shrink. Is that why you left the other night? You think you're better than us now?"

"No, but I can't just sit here—"

"That is it, isn't it?" Vic lowered his forehead in a challenging manner, coming mere inches away, nose-to-nose. Chris saw dark pockets around Vic's eyes. "Yeah, you think you're better than us. Our families have been through a lot, and you think you can just abandon them? You're not the only one with this condition. It's time you man up."

Chris stepped back and eyed Vic in a new light. "What do you mean, condition?"

"You know exactly what I mean. You're not the only one who can go back and see it all. I can see everything before my time came, before the fire in my warehouse, before everything changed. EVERYTHING! Why do you think we all sit here every night, recounting old stories of our glory days? Where do all those memories come from? It never dawned on you you might not be the only one?"

Vic laughed as looked over Chris's awestruck expression.

"You think you're better than us," Vic shook his head, "so unique, eh? Praeda was right. I thought I had a friend, but you're going to leave us and run away, just like you left your family. I saw what happened to my family after that fire and it all changed for me. And I'm not leaving them like you did yours. I will be here FOREVER, and you're not welcome inside these walls ever again. You had your chance and now you want to a redo because Jake is following in your footsteps? No. Jake is now in my family, not yours. Go wander the streets alone."

"No," Chris said firmly. He had heard enough and would not curl up and die. He would fight for what he wanted, fight for his son.

Chris boldly stepped forward and shoved Vic. Vic grabbed Chris's arm and brought him tumbling down with him.

Chris fell on Vic with his forearm on Vic's chest. Vic held Chris's shirt tight with one hand, and with his other hand, he shot jab-like uppercuts at Chris, peppering him with three firm blows to the side of his jaw.

Chris tucked his head in defense, taking it close to his chest as Vic's blows shifted from his jaw to brushing off the side of Chris's head. Chris's forearm had shifted from Vic's chest to pinning down his shoulder. As he gathered himself, he shifted his forearm from Vic's shoulder to his throat, forcing him to stop throwing punches in the close quarters as he gasped for air and squirmed. But Chris's weight on Vic's hips held tight. Vic choked and released Chris's shirt as he clawed at Chris's forearm.

The two bouncers came to Vic's rescue, both grabbing the smaller Chris and lifting him off of Vic.

Chris felt weightless as he floated off the ground, his eyes still locked on Vic as a knee met his left rib cage. He buckled over, holding his side. The men held their grip tight and a fist struck firmly into Chris's stomach, knocking out all the breath in his lungs.

Chris tried to spin away, to scramble toward the entrance. If he could only get Jake's attention. If he could only get through.

Another punch to Chris's stomach. His legs stopped churning and he sagged in pain. Another blow, aimed at his stomach but striking his sternum as he crumpled over.

The two men threw Chris toward the road. He bounced off a parking meter, feeling a shot of pain behind his shoulder, and landed across the unforgiving concrete curb.

Vic stood up, brushed himself off without a word, and walked back into the lounge.

The two bouncers motioned for the next in line to step forward.

No one in the waiting crowd seemed to notice, or care, as Chris rolled in pain and tried to stand.

Chapter Seven

Downstream Effects

Chris hobbled away from the lounge and toward his old home. Evelyn must be there; he could talk to her. She could get ahold of Jake. The injuries slowed Chris down, doubling the time it normally took to get to his old house, but as he walked, they subsided. No permanent damage was done.

He banged on the front door the moment he arrived, a stark contrast to how he had left quietly years ago, but no answer. He tried the handle, locked. And he didn't have the key.

Walking around the side of the house, he found Evelyn on the screened-in back porch that overlooked the backyard. Her normally well-kept hair looked frazzled and loose, not held back in her typical ponytail or bun. Chris could see the redness in and around her eyes. She had been crying.

As Chris approached, she nervously picked up her cell phone, checking for messages and putting it back down. He watched her carefully as she wrung her hands together. Her unconscious nervous tic of squeezing her palms and pulling her fingers. She always did that when she was unsure or scared, but didn't want to show it. He hadn't seen her fret like this since before he left. Stepping forward, he opened his mouth, but Evelyn's phone rang before he got a word out. Evelyn snatched it quickly and stood up, turning away from Chris and pacing behind the ornamental iron bench that centered on the porch.

"He never came home from school and his coach said he wasn't at practice. This isn't like him," Evelyn said into the phone.

Chris cautiously stepped forward, not wanting to startle her.

"I've been trying. His phone is off. Is there anyone else you can think of? Anywhere else?" she questioned. "They said he was at school." She paused again and Chris stepped closer, only a few steps away from the door to the porch.

"I did, several times. You know that woman never answers her phone, though, ever since Vic..." She paused and swallowed. Chris could tell she was holding back tears. "...I'll try again though. Maybe she'll get off whatever it is she's on this time. The coach said that was the only other boy who missed practice. They have to be together."

Chris softly opened the screen door and gently closed it behind himself. The door was silent and smooth except for the loud closing. It always made a loud bang when the latch returned and snapped back into place.

The loud bang surprised Evelyn as she turned and looked toward Chris. He put his hands up tightly to his chest, showing his palms.

"I just want to help. I saw him," Chris spoke.

Evelyn let the phone drift down below her shoulder as the person on the other end continued talking. She looked curiously toward Chris as if accepting he had something to say.

"He's at the lounge, with Vic's boy and some other kids. I just saw them."

Evelyn quickly turned, opening the sliding door into the living room. "What about the lounge?" she said rapidly into the phone. "Christian and Vic went there all the time. Why not their boys?"

"I know, I know he's only seventeen, but remember when we were in high school? They didn't always check our IDs too hard, did they?" She rushed toward the kitchen and grabbed her purse and car keys off the counter as she listened.

"Okay, you keep calling around. I can get there quickly and will keep you posted. Love you too, Sis."

Evelyn trotted toward the front door and turned back toward the porch before walking out. "I'm coming with you," Chris said. He noticed she wasn't wringing her hands anymore.

———◆◇◆———

The car ride was silent as Evelyn sped in her white SUV through the neighborhood streets toward the strip of stores and restaurants that rested on the outskirts of downtown. In only minutes, she covered what took a wounded Chris nearly an hour to walk.

She parked on the side of the road and moved swiftly through the entrance. She moved with a determined purpose, like a mama bear hearing her cub call for her. If Chris didn't know any better, he would have sworn she worked there or owned the place, the way she moved through the crowd. The bouncers ignored her as they dealt with the packed lines of the young crowd, eagerly starting their nightlife.

Chris needed to get inside to help Evelyn, to find Jake, but knew causing another scene in front of the entrance wouldn't help anyone. He noticed a flickering light down the small strip plaza and trotted down the street to get a closer look. A tight alley waited in the flickering street lamp between the shop at the end of the strip and a tall wooden fence. He moved into the tight space and around crates and small dumpsters scattered behind the building. Turning the corner, he saw a few cars parked behind the building and back entrance doors for each of the shops. He jogged up to a bright light that illuminated an area on either side of the lounge's back entrance. He could hear music coming through the crack in the door. It was unlocked and propped open with a small book wedged between the door and the frame.

As Chris moved quietly toward the door, the small book's white cover contrasted with the dirt and grime of the alley and doorway. Somehow, the book remained clean, a flawless white, like it has a non-stick surface, and small gold letters on the pocket-sized book read *The New Testament*.

Chris crept in and slunk through the back hallway and kitchen without being seen, popping out near the bathrooms and sidebar area of the busy lounge. He peered through the shoulder-to-shoulder crowd as he cautiously advanced, not wanting to end up in another skirmish or worse, drawing Praeda's attention.

He saw Vic and the other regulars in their corner. Vic was sitting in Chris's old spot and carrying on the conversation, capturing the attention of everyone at the table, and the boys were nowhere around.

Finally, he caught sight of Evelyn. She was pleading with a young waitress, who looked too busy to reply. As the waitress picked up four buckets of beer, she finally turned and replied to Evelyn. They spoke a moment, Evelyn leaning her ear close to the waitress's mouth to hear through the deafening noise of the crowd. Evelyn looked hopeful, but a moment later, her shoulders dropped. She asked a few more questions, and the waitress took her turn, leaning in to hear.

Before the waitress could respond again, Chris saw Praeda slide over to the slide of the bar and holler at her. His large hands made a shooing motion and the waitress immediately responded in kind, shooing away Evelyn as she went back to her work.

Evelyn moved back toward the entrance, leaving the lounge, and Chris weaved through the crowd, following closely behind. By the time Chris made it through the crowd and snuck past the bouncers who were so focused on the front door, they could not have cared less about monitoring the exit door behind them. Evelyn was already in her car. Chris trotted up to the driver's side window and saw she was rubbing her eyes.

"Go home, Ev. I'll find him," he shouted through the car window. "I promise. I'll find him. Go home and wait for him."

Evelyn took a deep breath and looked up at the roof of her car as she blinked, trying to clear her watery eyes. "Okay, okay," she said, not looking toward Chris, "I have to trust you with this. I won't stop seeking, but I will trust you. Bring him home, Lord, PLEASE bring him home safe."

As she put her keys in the ignition, he backed away from the car. "I love you, Evelyn. I'll bring him home."

He saw her shoulders rise and fall slowly with a calming breath before she pulled away. Chris watched the taillights fade before they pulled around a corner and went out of sight.

Looking around the crowd to his right and the empty town in all other directions, he did not know where to start. He'd just promised his wife he'd find their son, and all he knew was where they were hours ago. He failed to get Jake's attention then; why did he think he could find him now, let alone get his attention? Evelyn barely looked at him.

But a piece of hope kept with him, something Michael said to him from sessions ago: "Just show up." He may have failed before by being distant husband and lacking father since his accident, but his resolve was strengthening. He was trying to get better with every session with Michael and it was showing: he fought to see Jake, then he went to Evelyn for the first time in years, and then snuck around the alley to find a way in the back of the lounge.

He was showing up, and there wasn't a chance in this whole sad world that he was going to stop now.

He'd look all night if he had to.

He would show up for his family. To do the right thing for them. He was finding his purpose for this stage of his life.

But where to start... He walked up and down the small strip plaza looking for a sign for a flickering light to guide him again, but nothing. The loud crowd in and outside the lounge drew his attention as it contrasted against the emptiness of the surrounding area.

He sat on the curb across the street and observed the crowd as he thought. "Where are you, Jake?" he said to himself.

His mind blank, he realized he was in the same spot as Evelyn's car before she pulled away. He remembered her praying before she left. It inspired him, and another sound bite from Michael rang in his head: "This is a Christian organization."

"All those Sundays in the pew." He sadly laughed to himself as he looked up at the night sky. "Is this what it all comes down to, a moment of need where I reach out to you?"

Chris felt frustrated, like a huge swell of pride was overtaking him, making him think he could do this on his own. He could figure it all out. It might take all night, but he would keep walking, exploring all the nearby areas, then making a bigger sweep. He could go down by the river, then by the school, then back behind the fields. He would hit all the hang-out spots he knew of, and then, if he needed to, he'd go right up to Vic's house and beat that door down until he got answers. But he wasn't walking, he wasn't on his way to all those spots. He was sitting on a damp curb, struggling over how to pray, fighting with his own pride about why he shouldn't be trusting God but trying to do it all himself.

He realized he was lying to himself. He could show up all he wanted, and he was happy about that. It had gotten him this far. But he knew he'd reached his limit. He couldn't run forever trying to find his boy.

Chris swallowed as he fought back his tears and envisioned himself pushing that prideful feeling back down through his belly and into the ground, out of his body.

"I have nothing left," he said as he bowed his head. "I need your help, Lord. Help me find Jake, help me keep him safe. I don't even have to find him if you keep him safe. Bring him home. Lord, let his mother know he's in your arms. Watch over my family like I failed to do, like only you could do. I have nothing in this world without you. I'm sorry...I'm sorry for wasting this life..."

Chris buried his face in his forearms as he wrapped his arms around his legs and curled up in a ball on the wet curb. "I'm sorry...Help me, Lord," he repeated.

His car accident flashed in his head, then the hospital afterward. He saw the husband of the family from the car next to him, down in a ball, crying in the hallway just like he was now. That man knew what he lost the moment it happened. It took Chris five years to realize it.

For the first time, he could remember every detail of a moment beyond his accident. Standing in the hospital, watching the man cry in the hallway, he saw himself in the man. He was on the hospital floor just like Chris was in his apartment bathroom, just like Chris was now on a damp curbside.

In shambles, lost, not knowing the next step. But praying.

Chris heard the man speak a prayer to God. Between the crying and sniffing, Chris heard him praying.

Chris stepped closer. "Thy kingdom come, Thy will be done," he heard. It struck Chris's heart. The frustration in the man's voice echoed in Chris's ears as his tears turned to spittle as he spoke. "Thy kingdom come. Thy will be done." He said again. "Thy kingdom. Thy will. Thy kingdom. Thy will."

This man lost everything, yet even in his lament, he was praying.

Then Chris heard a noise that pulled him away from the man; there were others crying behind him. He turned around to see a doorway into another hospital room. He walked closer to it. A sense of dread covered him and he was afraid to move in, but his feet unconsciously carried him.

A binder rested in a clear holder on the open door. He saw his name, written in black marker at the top of the paperwork.

The sobbing sounds grew louder as he moved through the doorway.

On the bed was a body, the blankets pulled up to cover the deceased person's face. A chill ran up his spine.

He turned to see Evelyn and Jake. It was a younger Jake, only twelve, held tight in his mother's arm. He was crying uncontrollably as he buried his head in his mother's chest, her blouse wet with tears.

Evelyn's chin rested on his head. She was trying to hold back tears, to tell her boy it was okay, but the tears were winning. The emotions were pushing through as she sobbed, rocking her son tight in her arms.

Chris watched Evelyn and Jake weep as they held on to each other, mourning the death of Christian.

Chapter Eight

Influence

Chris stood up from the damp curb and wiped his eyes. Then he finished his prayer, "Lord, I don't know why I'm here, but I'm here only because of you. Help me accomplish whatever it is you put me here to do. Work through me, Lord. I'm sorry for all that I've done, all the pain that I caused. For being so distant from my family, I'm sorry, yet...I'm thankful. Thank you for giving me every second of time with them. I didn't earn it; it was a gift. Thank you."

———◆O◆———

Lights flickered on in the area surrounding the lounge, lighting up other shops and the expansive parking lot to the left of the lounge entrance.

The parking lot.

What if Jake and his friends only left the lounge, but stayed in the parking lot?

Chris completed his prayer as his walk toward the lot turned into a jog. "Now let me be there for them, Lord. Thy kingdom come, thy will be done. Let it be *your* will, not mine." He began running. "It's not about me anymore."

He ran into the large lot. The size of the lot always surprised him when it was nearly empty in the early evening hours, but now with cars packing the lot, he stopped wondering about the size and thought of the best way to go through it. A car swung around the corner as he turned to start down one row. He jumped back to avoid it and noticed three boys in the car, each about Jake's age. He couldn't make out what they were talking about as they whipped by with their windows up, but he could see the boy in the back seat was sitting next to a set of golf clubs.

A car was backing up as he turned down the aisle. He rushed over as it shifted out of reverse and rolled forward. The windows were down and Chris saw the driver trying to light a cigarette before pulling away.

"Here, you want one," the driver said as Chris could see the passenger take the pack from the driver's hand.

Chris bent down and saw the driver was Vic's son, Louis. The passenger was Jake.

"Jake!" Chris shouted. "Your mother is worried. GO HOME! Be with her."

Jake's head turned slightly, twitching at the sound of a distant voice. "No, thanks," he responded to his friend, passing back the pack as the car quickly pulled away. It spun its tires as it quickly made the turn out of the parking lot.

Chris noticed a bag of golf clubs in the back seat of their car as well. Why would they have clubs in the middle of the night? He walked out of the parking lot and toward the road, seeing tail lights fade in the distance.

"Golf at night?" he questioned himself as he looked around. He saw two guys who stumbled out of the lounge kick an empty can around as they playfully pushed each other to have the next turn. It took his attention as he thought about the two: Two mid-twenty-something guys, in the middle of the night, still trying to play sports and be competitive.

Then he realized it. He knew what Jake and his friends were doing, but where? He flashed back to a memory from before his accident and found the place.

Chris took off at a steady, well-paced jog, determined to keep his promise to Evelyn. Determined to find Jake.

———◦———

Less than twenty minutes later, Chris turned the corner into the softball and little league fields. Four fields and a small kids' playground sat next to the woods of a small preserve, isolated from nearby subdivisions. Signs stating the area was closed past

10:00 pm with nightly patrols betrayed what everyone knew: police never patrolled the park. It was the perfect place to make noise and be wild for a drunk teenager in the middle of the night.

Before Chris's accident, at a softball game during warmups, he found a pile of golf balls scattered around left field. He nearly rolled his ankle when he stepped on one as he threw pop flies to his centerfielder. Mentioning it to the team back in the dugout, a few of the younger guys on the team commented they would come out some nights after sneaking out to the bar to hit golf balls at the backstop. The younger kids were now older and carrying on the tradition.

As Chris approached the complex, he heard an occasional rattle of the chain-linked backstop and the cheering that followed. All five boys from the two cars were in the outfield of the little league field.

He walked directly toward Jake, passing by two young men that stumbled and fell after missing their swings. Lying on the ground inebriated, they laughed and showed no desire to get up and hit the ball again. A third boy sat in the grass, looking up at the stars and howling like a wolf whenever a well-struck ball shook the backstop.

Louis and Jake were going swing for swing. The white golf balls and twelve-pack of reflective beer cans stood out in the dim light surrounding their feet. The ping of a well-struck ball grew louder in Chris's ear as he approached, the impact of a ball hitting the backstop echoed.

Getting close to the two, Chris saw a third person standing close to Louis. He walked closer and saw it was a man talking to Louis.

"Don't let this fairy beat you. Come on, swing harder! Hit it over the entire field! Why'd you bring a 9-iron out? You should have brought the six. Stupid. Come on, son! Blast that thing!"

"Vic? What are you doing here?"

Vic turned to Chris, surprised to see him at the fields. "I told you, I got the boys. It's not your place anymore." Walking around Louis, Vic came up behind Jake. "Come on now, you can hardly drink. Let's see what you can do off the tee. I'm surprised you can even make contact—"

Chris interrupted Vic and stepped in between him and Jake. "Get away from my son!"

"Oh, now you care. You act like this is the first time." Vic waved his hands toward the other boys and the field. "Where were you last year when they lost districts in overtime? When your loser kid had the turnover that cost them the game? Huh?"

"I..." Chris hesitated.

"Yeah, that's what I thought. You no-show for years. Now, suddenly you pop back up. Well, too late." Vic approached Chris with an aggressive stance, just like he had earlier that night at the lounge entrance. "I saw you at the lounge nearly every night. You knew our kids hung out together. And how many times did you show up at their games? Watch them practice? Or even ASK ME about him?"

Chris dropped his head, ashamed.

"Exactly," Vic repeated before turning back to Jake and Louis. "You had your chance and you blew it. All your little walks past your old place, you were too much of a punk to go in and handle your situation like a man. I DON'T CARE what happened to us. I'm not letting go or going anywhere! My kid will grow up to be a man, and if it takes turning your little loser into a man too, so be it. You're welcome."

Chris clenched his fists as his shame turned to rage. Vic was taller and stronger, but Chris's fury was building. He envisioned himself punching Vic right in the jaw. Not letting up. This fool was calling him weak, calling his only son a loser, and trying to berate him into some misguided form of manhood. Chris would show Vic exactly what he thought of his plan for Jake.

Chris leaned forward and cocked back his fist, ready to unload, but then he saw Jake turn toward Louis.

"Hey, quit taking from my pile," Jake said directly.

"Oh please, I brought all these balls, loser," Louis responded, mimicking his father as he picked up an open can and swigged the drink.

"Yeah, and I brought the beer." Jake dropped his club and stood facing Louis in a challenging stance.

Louis turned his head to look above Jake and blew out all the beer in a spray above them. "There, you can have it back." He dropped his club and stepped forward.

Vic noticed the standoff and egged Louis on. "Going to teach this loser a—"

"DON'T call my son a loser!" Chris interrupted as he closed the gap toward Vic.

Jake followed suit and stepped closer to Louis. Chris noticed his son clench his fist, just like his own hand.

Then it dawned on Chris. The boys were mirroring their fathers' aggression toward each other.

Chris could swing on Vic all he wanted, and Jake would do the same toward Louis. What would that prove?

"Come on, cry baby. No one here to separate us this round." Vic pushed up the sleeves on his skin-tight black shirt as he eyed Chris. The black bags under his eyes that Chris had noticed at the lounge were larger than before, more pronounced. They pulsed with Vic's growing anger.

"No," Chris said defiantly as his fists relaxed. "I'm not giving you this."

Vic laughed. "Oh yeah, be the bigger man, but really, you are a scared little punk, just like your son. I know why he's quiet and distant all the time. He's just like his punk father."

Vic pushed Chris, but Chris held firm, holding like a wall built on a rock foundation. Chris saw the glint of surprise in Vic's eye that he couldn't move the smaller man.

As Chris held his ground, it all made sense. Jake was mimicking Chris, even when he moved out. He became cold, now leaving his mother to sneak out to the lounge. It was everything Chris did when he faced his own doubt—hid in his memories—unable to move on from them.

"We're leaving," Chris said calmly as he turned away.

Jake turned as well. "This is dumb. I'm out of here."

Surprised, Louis fired back, "Good, I'd rather hit by myself than with some loser, anyway. And I'm keeping all your beer!"

"Good, take it," Jake said calmly as he began walking, lockstep with his father.

Louis tilted the bottom of his open can up and finished it, spiking it to the ground as bits of foam shot up in response.

Vic stepped in Chris and Jake's direction, ensuring his insults were the last word. "Yeah, walk away when things get tough. Go hide!"

Chris spoke firmly, without turning back. "No, Vic, for the first time, I'm not hiding."

Vic exhaled loudly, blowing off the comment. "What kind of man are you, anyway?"

"No better than you, but God-willing, we're better off," Chris said softly to himself as he looked at Jake. Proud of the boy. Proud of himself.

Chris and Jake walked the miles home together in silence. Chris was proud of his son for walking away. He could see Jake's feeling of shame for lying to his mother, for ignoring her, and no words needed to be said about the mistakes the boy made that night. As they walked, Chris sensed a feeling of peace within them both, a sense of belonging and calmness.

Evelyn shot up from her restless sleep on the living room couch the moment she heard the front door.

She ran to Jake and hugged him tightly. "Thank you, thank you, thank you, thank you, thank you," she repeated as she held her son.

Chris moved in, wrapping his arms around both of them. "I'm sorry. I love you both so much. I'm so sorry."

He felt more peace and love at that moment than any memory from his lifetime.

Chapter Nine

Once You See...

Chris strolled home that night with a smile painted on his face that he could not hide, even if he wanted to. He hugged Jake and Evelyn, holding them tightly and feeling the powerful love of their family. By the way Jake and Evelyn held each other tight, he could tell they felt it too.

Jake and Evelyn soon went to bed, and Chris took the cue to walk home. He felt lighter on his feet, and love filled his heart as the pain from the fight outside the lounge was nearly gone. He began thinking about how he would describe the night to Michael in their next session.

As he walked up the concrete stairs of his apartment complex, dew from the night was making the early morning air damp and cool. He began singing a tune he hadn't heard in years. He hummed along to the tune is his head, not caring if he remembered the words in the correct order. He sang as some of the words came back to him, loud and out of tune, but as joyful as could be as he beat imaginary drums with his index fingers in front of him.

He abruptly stopped singing when he got to his door and noticed it was half open. The deadbolt was still engaged, sticking out from behind a splintered wood frame. Someone fiercely kicked the door open, shattering the frame.

Cautiously pushing the door open, he slowly advanced inside.

Walking through the tiny entrance hallway and into the living room, he found Praeda and Vic sitting comfortably on his couch as if long-lost friends awaiting Chris's arrival.

"Ah! Welcome, my friend," Praeda said, holding out his arms but not getting up from Chris's worn-out love seat.

"I don't think friends kick in each other's doors," Chris responded as he looked from Praeda to Vic.

"You cannot expect us to wait outside in that hallway. Your hand-me-down furniture is bad enough." Praeda flicked a large piece of fuzz off the shabby armrest of the small couch before standing up. He towered over Chris, and his broad upper body blocked the streetlight coming through the window like an eclipse. Praeda's colossal frame dominated the small room. He still looked like he could compete in a Strong Man competition, or take on ridiculous feats of strength, like pulling a school bus through a parking lot as effortlessly as Chris might walk a dog.

"You know, Chris, I feel hurt by you avoiding my lounge lately. We are a family and families stick together, especially ones in such situations." He motioned to Chris and then to Vic. "You each want to be there for your own families, and I get that, but we cannot forget about the bond we forge with consistent gathering among us who suffer. This world is a hard and lonely place.

You worked your whole life and what do you have to show for it? A house that sits miles away, owned by your past life? Paying rent for a crappy apartment that you'd be ashamed to show anyone? You don't have to keep fighting against yourself. You can find solace in the lounge, with those just like you, in sharing the memories of your life with others."

"By living in the past?" Chris asked.

"By learning from it, by discussing it, by exploring it." Praeda put his hands up in the air as if exploring the stars. "All that you experienced, tell others about it as you rest your soul. I've worked hard to provide a place for all types of people to come and find comfort, to find their people. Don't turn your back on it so you can run in circles."

"You have it all wrong, Praeda," Chris said.

"Oh, do I? You have no idea how long I've been building this, yet you have one disagreement," he motioned to Vic, who remained silent, "and you think you know it all." He laughed. "You belong to me more than you know. You've been here for what? A whole five seconds? Please, enlighten me."

"You said I need a place to rest, a place to go to talk about my past. But no, it's not about that anymore. IT'S NOT ABOUT ME. Not anymore," Chris said boldly.

Praeda's face tightened into a stern glare toward Chris as his welcoming attitude washed away.

"It's not about my past, it's about *their* future." Chris pointed toward his family's home. "They cannot move on with me still around. I have been selfish, and I didn't escape to the lounge to grow smarter from my past; I went to hide from my future. I see that now, and once you see, you cannot unsee."

"You're even talking like him now." Praeda rolled his eyes in disgust. "Thankfully, there is a wide road of people that walk toward me and only a few misguided souls follow the narrow path. The subservient nonsense that has brainwashed you and all the others that eventually move on from here."

Praeda turned and looked out the window, placing two large fingers in between the cheap plastic blinds and pulling them apart. "You know it won't last, right?"

Chris didn't respond, waiting for Praeda to continue.

"All this 'serve others', 'move on to a better place', and the rest of that lovely-dovey nonsense. I thought you were smarter than all that, but despite your disrespect, I have not lost faith in you. You'll see...Michael's lies of 'just showing up' keep getting buried under more pursuit. If you are so enlightened, so saved, then why do you need to keep working for it? If it is so natural, then why doesn't it come easier? It doesn't add up and only leads to him controlling you. You become a slave. Chris, this world, right here, right now, your situation, is for *YOU*."

"Stop calling me Chris."

Praeda ignored Chris's comments. "You can do this the easy way or the hard way. You think you know it all, but you'd be amazed if you could see the lies for what they really are. You run from your sadness and fears that we can help you understand. Stay with me and learn. Chris, this—"

"I said, STOP calling me Chris. *YOU* can call me Christian."

"I see..." Praeda said sadly. "If I cannot welcome you into the gates of my city, then you are a threat." He looked toward Vic and, on cue, Vic stood up and cracked his knuckles. "But dealing with threats can be fun too."

Christian noticed Praeda's face lose all signs of friendliness. A sinister smile broke across his face as deep, black bags formed under Praeda's eyes. Praeda stepped forward as Vic also closed in on Christian. They herded him into the thin, six-foot entrance hallway. Vic moved quickly, but Christian paused. The look on Vic's face caught him by surprise. The black bags and menacing expression on Praeda's face seemed to transfer to Vic as they looked more and more alike.

Vic lunged forward, hooking his left hand toward Christian's face. Christian turned, but not fast enough as Vic's fist caught his jaw. Vic then threw his right hand, burying it in Christian's stomach as he stepped closer. Christian fought back. From his hunched-over position, he threw an upper-cut that landed firmly on Vic's chin.

As Vic stumbled back, Praeda stepped forward with a powerful jab that caught Christian's left cheekbone. Christian could fight off Vic, but Praeda's blow was on another level. He could not go toe-to-toe with Praeda. The powerful blow was like a sledge-hammer and it knocked Christian back into his entrance hallway. Falling through the open door behind him, he expected to land hard on the concrete hallway floor.

But he didn't smack down on the concrete. He landed comfortably in a set of large, powerful arms that held him safely and brought him back up to his feet. Dazed by Praeda's shot, Christian blinked and looked up.

It was Michael.

He wore the same style outfit that Christian was used to seeing him in, but something was different about him. He had a glow that emanated strength, yet he had a comfort about it. Even with Vic and Praeda still in his apartment, Christian felt safe.

Michael looked down and smiled like it was an ordinary night, like he just bumped into Christian in the hallway. "Hello, Christian. It is good to see you."

Turning his head to peer into Christian's apartment, Michael lost his smile as his face hardened and his gaze locked on Praeda.

Praeda snarled, and Vic got back to his feet, standing behind him. Praeda's fingers twitched as he repeatedly made fists with his hands and then released the tight squeeze. He was a bull ready to charge at Michael.

Michael stepped into the doorway, having to crouch down to fit. His massive frame now filled Christian's entrance. Christian watched him move through the doorway and noticed a small book in Michael's back pocket. It was bright white and seemed to radiate like Michael. The pocket-sized New Testament, the same one that held the back-door of the lounge entrance open.

Over Michael's hunched-over shoulders, Christian could see Praeda and Vic. Vic stepped back, away from Michael as Praeda stood his ground. The dark expression coming over Praeda counteracted the warm glow that Michael gave off. The large black bags under his eyes appeared to bleed across his entire face and then over his body as he seemed to absorb any surrounding light. He was a black hole facing a sun that would not give up its space.

Praeda's angry snarl only deepened as Michael approached. Christian was used to seeing Praeda's size and popping muscles physically dominate a room, dwarfing anyone who stood close to him. But not compared to Michael. Praeda looked smaller, weaker, in the presence of Christian's sponsor.

Christian expected his apartment to be torn apart by the two but was surprised as Michael spoke calmly to Praeda, holding out a hand. "You are still welcome. You are still loved, my brother."

The comment only fueled the hateful fire burning inside Praeda. The black aura around him seemed to pulse off his skin as his fury grew. He stepped forward toward Michael, but Michael was ready and responded in kind, now standing tall to his full height as the tiny hallway opened up to higher ceilings.

But Praeda didn't attack.

He didn't challenge Michael and rip apart Christian's apartment in a furious melee.

With a snarl, Praeda turned and ran, with Vic following. In a flash, they were out the second floor patio and bounding down the fire escape. Michael watched them go, not giving chase.

After a moment of silence, he turned and hugged Christian. "I'm proud of you."

Chapter Ten

Bigger Picture

The next day, Christian and Michael met for their typical session, but somehow everything was different. Christian felt different, reborn, as if he was a totally new person with a changed perspective. An enormous bruise covered the left side of his face where Praeda had struck him. While the injury looked painful, it didn't bother Christian. The wound was his reminder of standing up to Vic and Praeda, and even though it was Michael who ultimately saved him, Christian felt he had done his part. He stayed afloat amongst the trials of the night. He stayed afloat long enough for Michael to pull him out of the dark, rough waters.

As he walked into the dimly light gymnasium, Michael stood waiting under the emergency lights. He smiled as Christian approached.

"Hello, Christian," Michael greeted.

"Hello," Christian responded, mirroring Michael's smile.

"No chairs?" Christian questioned as he realized their normal space was not set up.

"Not today. Follow me," Michael began walking toward a back hallway of the gym. A bright light that crept through a door frame somewhere in the back of the hallway illuminated. The thin light stretched against the shadows of the dimly light gymnasium. It reached across the floor as if marking their path.

"I've never noticed that light before. Was it always back here?" Christian asked.

"Yes, it is always here. Sometimes it is hard to see, but ultimately, it shines for everyone who comes through here."

They walked in silence as Christian thought about the night before. He thought about finding Jake, about seeing his actions impact his son's actions, and about hugging Jake and Evelyn.

"Tell me," Michael interrupted the silence, "what was most useful for you here?"

Christian took a deep breath as he gathered his thoughts. He already knew his answer to Michael's question, but finally, he accepted it and verbalized it. "The crying father...Seeing him mourn his family, knowing that I caused that," Christian's heart sank. "But...but honestly, if it *had* to happen, I'm glad I saw him. He helped me finally realize how awful I can be. I think I was a good husband, a solid dad, but I was drifting. I was aimless, and my son was right behind me. But seeing him...it made me feel awful, yet...thankful, all at once. It made me realize I need a foundation, a firm base; otherwise, I probably would still be in the lounge every night. And Jake would probably be there right next to me."

Michael nodded. "Thank you for sharing that."

"You, and this place." Christian put up his arms. "You became my foundation. You saved me. Thank you."

Michael turned and smiled at Christian. "You are a great man. Evelyn and Jake know that too, and I am pleased he chose me to work with you."

"You say it like this is over?"

"Only a new beginning." Michael nodded and looked Christian in the eyes as one hand motioned toward the light coming from the hallway. "This is our last session together."

"I'm going to miss our time together," Christian accepted, "and if I know what is through those doors, then I'm going to miss Evelyn and Jake as well."

"You can stay and watch them, if you choose. The accident that brought you here was not fully your choice, but the next step is. It's *your* choice here."

Turning back to Michael, Christian asked, "My condition, how I can remember everything before my accident, it isn't that rare, is it?"

Michael shook his head. "No. It is part of the choice, a part of understanding. It helps many, but others...Well, let's just say others find it tougher to move on."

"Like Vic?"

Michael nodded yes. "Praeda uses that to his advantage."

"I'm not supposed to stay here, am I?"

"That is up to you, Christian."

"I thought I would be scared, but...I'm not."

"When you are ready, you are simply...ready. Like your marriage to Evelyn, or having Jake."

"I wish I could remember all these moments, our talks, that last hug with Evelyn and Jake. I wish I could take those with me."

"Think of it this way, Christian. Your life was one brushstroke of vibrant color within a masterpiece, and *this* place a flick of the wrist to give it texture, to raise your paint up off the canvas. From your raised view of that final flick, you see your original stroke better. You see your life, from start to finish, in all its wonderful detail. But *this* place is only a fraction of the total view, whereas the *next* place...well, in the next place, you are not limited to viewing only your stroke or where your paint blends with others close to you. You see the full painting in all its glory and splendor. You and your family are all a part of the masterpiece."

Christian nodded as they began walking toward the hallway. The light grew brighter as they approached.

"Can I ask you one more question?" Christian said, turning to Michael.

"Of course."

"What happened to that family?" He looked down in shame, but quickly brought his head back up to meet Michael's eyes. "The one from my accident. What happened to them?"

Michael opened his arms and hugged Christian. Christian never felt a hug like that. Michael held him so tight, so warm, so safe. It reminded him of hugging Jake and Evelyn the night before, filled with love.

Stepping back from the embrace and holding Christian's arms in his large hands, Michael slowly said, "They moved on. Just like you." With a smile and a soft nudge toward the light of the hallway, Michael's hands dropped.

Christian walked into the hallway, the light growing brighter and brighter as he approached the door.

Reaching out his hand, he took the handle and held it tight. With a deep breath, he turned the knob and walked through.

The End.

Thank You and Free Preview!

This is James Bonk, the author, and I want to thank you for reading *Christian's Look Back at Life* by giving you the first chapter of **Light of the Ark**, the first book in the Light of the Ark series, you can purchase it here: https://store.jamesbonk.com/ and use code BESTSELLER to get 15% off!

I hope you enjoy it.

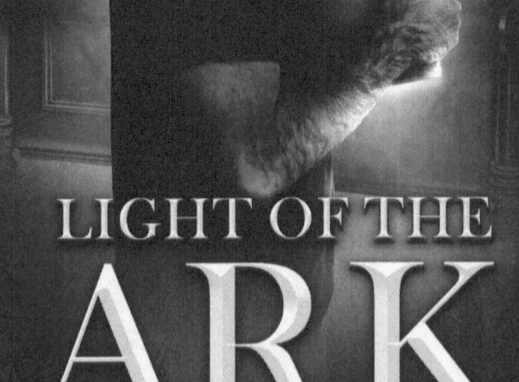

JAMES BONK

LIGHT OF THE
ARK

Book 1 of Light of the Ark series

Coffee with Dad

The steam from the coffee rose before his face as he stared, lost in thought. He was inches away from taking a sip, but his mind was captured before he could.

"Dad."

He wasn't here; his mind was somewhere else.

"Dad..."

His eyes were locked on the Bible on the end table next to him. It was an old Bible but had held up well. The thick green covers were tattered from wear, but it was handled with care for the decades or more it had been in the family's possession. Even with the wear, it always had sort of a glow to it, a welcoming and unique nature. Recent events added deep cuts into the hard green backing, and the spine of the book was half torn off, now held by a strip of grey duct tape. Matthew knew more about the story and the book, but far from all of it. That would take a lifetime.

"Dad. You okay?"

The funeral was yesterday. All of the boys, along with their wives and kids, had packed into the old home they grew up in. Zechariah had three boys: Luke, Mark, and Matthew. Each of them had two kids. The extra twelve in Zech and Mary's home was a strain, but a welcome one to the heads of the Light family. Each son had offered to put his family in a hotel, or in Matthew's case, drive the hour and stay in their own home, but their mother wouldn't hear of it. Secretly, all of the boys liked being back in their old home. The sons, wives, and grandparents could all have breakfast together, play games in the backyard, and stay up late playing cards after the kids went down. That sort of family time does not happen when part of the family wakes up in a hotel twenty minutes away.

Back when the boys were young, the house was busy, loud, and all-around hectic. Now that their kids were here, it brought back those chaotic memories. The grandkids ranged from diapers to high school and thankfully all got along and played well with each other.

"Hey, Grandpa!"

Matthew's oldest daughter's voice snapped Zech out of his trance before Matthew's words could. The aged patriarch smiled at the five-year-old to acknowledge her. She thanked him for the bacon but now was eager for her grandfather's famous pancakes. He loved making his grandkids bacon, especially the real pork kind, as well as blueberry pancakes. Zech's wife Mary made nearly every meal in that house since they were married, but once a week and on special occasions, Zech made bacon and pancakes. Mary would talk with the kids and grandkids while sipping on her coffee, and Zech worked away in the kitchen, usually singing along to various country songs. The house picked up the wonderful smell of bacon. The smell rolled through the house and Zech's ear-to-ear grin was nearly as contagious as the hunger.

This morning was different, though. The funeral lingered in the air while recent events weighed on Matthew's and Zech's minds.

The artifact, as they had come to call it, was paramount, but for different reasons.

The crate.

Jeremiah.

Terrence.

Isaiah.

Even Micah loomed in their thoughts. That was new for Matthew, but not for Zech, as Micah had been a daily thought for nearly three decades.

As more grandkids ran past, Zech looked to his son, finally acknowledging him.

"Paul stopped by last night while you and Liz were out. He asked for us to come by the yard today. He and I both want to talk with you about the other night. The situation with Terrence."

"Dad, I already told the cops everything, and honestly, I am sick of talking about Terrence," Matthew replied. His voice echoed his frustration, but he kept it low with the kids nearby.

"You have learned more about your family and our responsibilities than I ever thought you would. There is much more to this than you know. And, honestly, I'm glad it is you that will be taking over."

Matthew stared at his dad, trying to get a read on him. Zech was not a huge man, but strong in his days, and he still carried a presence with him. The sort of presence that you respected, physically and spiritually. Matthew did not know what his father meant, but given the past two months, he knew it was serious.

Zech had pastored the church for decades, just as his father Isaiah did before him, as did his father... and his. None of his three sons were going to be the next pastor. Mark, the middle son, worked with the church, but as a missionary, currently based in Eastern Europe. Zech had flown

Mark, his wife, and two kids in for the funeral. Zech still mentored Mark and saw the kids on video calls weekly. Mark never saw himself as a pastor, and while he always attended, he did not work in the church for most of his twenties. He made his own path in finance and eventually tech investing, advising on IPOs and amassing a small fortune in his mid-twenties. However, he gave it all up, sold his shares in numerous companies that became tech giants, and moved into ministry. His small fortune could have been quite a large one if he had held on for only a few short years longer, but nope. Mark cashed out and never looked back. He never told Matthew the full reason, but his brothers knew. The week before Mark quit, he was on a trip with a few young and soon-to-be billionaires. He was being courted to help with their next IPO. The trip took a few detours, though, and Mark realized the slippery slope he was tip-toeing. His clients convinced the pilots of the private flight to divert the plane towards Vegas. Mark spent two nights trying to deal with the events, to just get through, but on the third day, enough was enough. He did not reboard the original flight and never looked back.

Luke was the oldest and lived a few hundred miles away in Atlanta. He loved the church and was a member at a sister location in Atlanta, but never showed interest in leading the church his father spent his life growing. Luke had had a rebellious childhood, mixing in with the wrong crowd and keeping his mother up many late nights during his teenage years. He took the long road, but eventually, after moving out and no longer getting financial support from his parents, Luke started building a new life. He rose up in the ranks at a local car shop from part-time work to becoming the right-hand man of the owner. Within a few years, Luke opened his own shop, and within another ten years, he owned a successful regional chain based in Atlanta. Matthew could see his father's work ethic and his mother's kindness in both of his brothers, and it served them well in their professional and personal lives.

The family torch to lead the church would have fallen onto Matthew, if it had not been for Jeremiah, Matthew's best friend who was practically a fourth son. Zech had been childhood friends with Jeremiah's father, Micah. When Micah passed away in his thirties, Jeremiah was only six years old, and Zech took it on himself to be Jeremiah's father-figure.

"J," as he had been called since he was a kid, fit in perfectly with the family. He and Matthew had been best friends their whole lives. The three Light boys were all above average height and played sports growing up, and J fit right in. J fit right in with the older boys as well, as he always seemed to be an inch or two taller and ten to twenty pounds heavier than Matthew. He could join one of Mark's teams without friends knowing he was younger, whereas Matt was obviously the youngest.

J took more to reading and noticed when Zech always had the Bible out. While

Matthew took a love of math into the engineering field, and J took a love of reading into scripture. The time in scripture at such a young age led him to become a Bible competition finalist and champion numerous times throughout grade school. By the time he was sixteen, he was filling in for the youth pastor and giving guest sermons to his peers in the youth groups.

Childhood memories of J and himself flashed in Matthew's mind as he took his turn getting lost in thought. The steam from his coffee began to fade in the cool morning air.

The thoughts of long-ago good times with his friend began to fade, and the past two months came into focus. Matthew could see J talking with Terrence after the Christmas Eve service.

Why did he not insist on finding out more?

He saw the look on J's face as he walked away from Terrence.

There were plenty of chances, but he figured his friend was fine. "He would say something. He's fine." Matthew heard his past self say it, over and over.

If he had only known then all the damage and the subsequent death that would come.

He could have helped.

He should have helped.

He would have helped! If he only knew...

Zech brought him back from his spiraling thoughts.

"We'll head to Paul's after breakfast. He said he'll be at the yard all morning working on repairs from last week's damage. For now, it's time we get these kids some pancakes before they mutiny on us."

Matthew and his wife Elizabeth, who went by Liz, had always been close to his parents. They enjoyed visiting for their own sake but mostly for their two girls. Grandma was their best friend and the only person Matthew knew who could out-energy a five-year-old. From a tea party, to freeze tag, into the pool, out of the pool, to another tea party, to story time, and on and on. Those kids slept great at their grandparents' house.

The adults would stay up late playing Euchre or Sequence or just talking, but soon would pass into a deep sleep just like the girls. The peacefulness of the house always took over.

Matthew and Liz had been married over ten years now. Liz's father, Paul Stollard, ran the Storage Yard just outside of town near the river. Paul was a little older than Zech and was almost like an older brother to him. They had been family friends for as long as Zech could remember. The Stollards regularly came to church, but being an hour away from the grounds, they did not always attend all the functions and events. That was a reason Matthew and Liz joked they should have met sooner.

Liz was a couple of years younger than Matthew. They could have met at a younger age but had a different circle of friends, attended different service times, and were in different youth groups. They had "known of" each other for years but went to different schools as kids. But then, at a mutual friend's party in college, they both delighted in seeing an old face from home and struck up a conversation. The friendship quickly turned into more, and from then on, they were inseparable and married less than two years later. Liz was a beautiful woman with amber-brown hair, bright brown eyes, and a picture-perfect smile. Matthew joked that she could grace the covers of any risqué men's magazine, yet he loved how she could dress conservatively and still be more desirable than any model in a low-cut shirt.

Liz was not only beautiful, but she was also Matthew's spiritual anchor. Without her, he likely would have drifted away from the church. With two young kids and living an hour away, it was easy to justify watching the message online or not at all. However, it was Liz who corralled the family and insisted they attend in person. It was so much easier to watch online, or better yet, simply listen to the audio version later in the week, but Liz would not have it, especially being the daughter-in-law to Pastor Zech and Mary. Liz knew they needed to be in person.

Matthew had been in church his whole life, but more out of habit than a burning desire. Once he moved out of his parent's house, the Sunday morning habit took a slight hit that snowballed into a low attendance rate, only attending during holidays or special events before dating Liz. He always felt like he was in the public eye as he passed through the rotunda and into the sanctuary each Sunday. His passive nature toward church bled into his professional life even after marrying Liz, more doing what he was told instead of proactively trying to help the company. His boss saw his potential—it flashed at times on big contracts where all of the company's leadership could not ignore it—however, it was few and far between. His boss gradually gave him more responsibility to flush out that potential, but the results were not reliable. Only in the past couple of months did his boss notice a change.

Being the youngest of three boys and having a best friend the size of his older brother, Matthew learned how to survive more than learning how to thrive. Unless he tried his absolute hardest, he did not have a shot in the backyard sports and games. Given the extra effort, he could hang with the larger boys, and it helped him best the majority of his peers; however, it also led to a fear of failure. Most new things he could succeed at, but eventually, there came a time when the effort waned and he stopped caring. It was all or nothing, and too often lately, he felt like nothing was winning, never putting in the work to carry his skills into mastery. Granted, his breadth in many sports and professional topics was immense, but he kept hitting the ceiling of his own burnout. Once he figured something out, he moved on. He feared his job at the engineering consulting company was coming to the same head. He was a licensed Professional Engineer for a private consulting company. He was brought in to help design manufacturing areas, warehouses, and office spaces, and then provide the simulations to show what tweaks could be made during build or later life to customize the space for optimum efficiency. He learned all the coding and visualization required to complete a seven-figure contract himself. However, where he really shined was when he put himself in the shoes of the workers who would one day inhabit the space. When that happened, he was a magnitude better than his old self. He would delegate the drawings and simulations, then critique and communicate with the team with ease as the project vastly improved from what he could do on his own. This was the potential his bosses saw, but unfortunately, Matthew seemed to randomly flash upward potential as opposed to consistently growing into the promotion he recently received.

But that all changed at the start of the new year. Two months ago, Matthew gradually showed the consistency his bosses desired. There was something growing in him. Something all the mentoring and training had not flushed out.

The family cleaned up the pancake breakfast, or what was left of it after the kids inhaled their meals. Matthew and his brothers decided to postpone their five-mile run into the woods, given Zech and Matthew's trip to see Paul and their now full bellies nearly putting them to sleep. Luke and Mark, along with their wives and Mary, moved into the backyard with the kids on the crisp morning. The ladies were planning a girls' trip to a few stores capped with lunch at the local Greek restaurant while the dads gathered the kids for a mix of football and tag. It looked more like Calvinball to Matthew as he turned from the back porch toward his father.

Matthew was glad the recent events, especially the funeral, were not weighing too hard on anyone as the day went on. Everyone except himself and his father. Both men took on a somber tone as the rest of the family moved away from breakfast. They quietly cleaned up the plates and silverware together. Zech's Bible now loomed heavy on Matthew's mind. It was one room away, but in his mind's eye, he could see it glowing.

The worn green Bible.

Decades old or more.

How it glowed bright in his mind.

As he began to ask his dad a question, Matthew paused when his cat, a fluffy grey Chartreux named Porkchop, jumped onto the front window seat. Recently, Matthew found himself talking to the cat more and more in the early morning hours. The cat, now ten years old, had been his confidant these past couple months. Matthew had a new appreciation for the feline and decided to bring him with them during the short stay at Zech and Mary's home.

He watched the cat as it stared back at him; with a slow blink, it moved its gaze to the front yard, seemingly directing Matthew to look. As Matthew looked through the front window, his grip on the used forks and knives turned white knuckle as his vision focused on what was outside on the front curb.

It was Terrence.

And he was holding a sledgehammer.

Terrence stared through the front window and his eyes met Matthew's. How long had he been out there? Did he watch them all eat breakfast or had he just pulled up?

Before Matthew could finish his thought, Terrence raised the sledgehammer, and with one smooth motion, brought it down like a meteor on the Lights' mailbox.

Matthew did not even notice the shotgun-like boom of the impact. He stared and thanked God the kids were in the backyard. Terrence then shot a look back at Matthew after the destruction, holding the gaze just as they locked eyes in the Storage Yard only days before when the muzzle of Terrence's shotgun was pointed into Matthew's chest.

Terrence then moved back into his car and was gone without another sound.

Matthew looked at the mailbox as his father came around from the kitchen. Zech asked what the noise was. The iron pole and box slouched, hunched over and pitiful after the blow, half as tall as it once was.

The family name "Light" now appeared scratched and shattered, hardly legible in the shadows of the bent iron.

You can purchase the Light of the Ark series here: https://store.jamesbonk.com/ and use code BESTSELLER to get 15% off!

Thank You!

I hope you enjoyed *Christian's Look Back at Life*.

Stay up to date on new releases and email exclusive content: https://hello.james-bonk.com/signup/

***

Tell the world and help readers like you find books like this:

Goodreads: https://www.goodreads.com/book/show/60766386 christian-s-look-back-at-life

***

I'd love to hear your thoughts, feedback, and questions. You can reach me at:

Email: jamesbonkwrites@gmail.com

Facebook: https://www.facebook.com/james.bonk.3154/

Books By James Bonk

<u>Light of the Ark Series</u>

1. Light of the Ark

2. Shadows of the Ark

3. Light of the World

- Isaiah and the Sea of Darkness (standalone prequel)

<u>More Fiction</u>

- Christian's Look Back at Life

Stay up to date on new releases and email exclusive content: https://hello.james-bonk.com/signup/

Acknowledgments

Thank you, Lord. None of this is possible without you.

My wife and daughters, for dealing with the extra time my mind spent in this world.

Leonard Petracci, for coaching me along this journey (*and for anyone who likes the Young Adult Sci-Fi / Urban Fantasy Genre, check out his work, especially the Star Child series*).

Pastor Russ and my Life Group brothers at Southpoint Community Church, for helping me think through these topics via sermons and weekly discussions.

Photographer, Author Picture: Alicia Bonk (https://aliciabonk.com/)

Cover Art Designer: Jelena Gajic (zelengajic@gmail.com)

Editing (Proofing): Beth Lynne (https://www.bzhercules.com/index.html)

The Author

James Bonk writes Christian Fiction to develop his own faith and as a ministry. He lives in the North Atlanta area with his wife, two daughters, and fluffy Chartreux cat, Porkchop. When he's not writing, he's usually swimming or building forts with his girls!

His Light of the Ark book was the #1 New Release in its category upon release, with multiple five star reviews from adults and young adults alike.

Besides writing, parenting, and being a husband, James Bonk is a supply chain leader and business intelligence professional. He has a BS in Mechanical Engineering, MS in Industrial Engineering, and an MBA. He previously held his Professional Engineering license in Industrial Engineering.

Find out more at and get access to all his books at:

https://store.jamesbonk.com/

You can also find James by searching James Bonk Author on your favorite platform or following the below links:

- Goodreads (https://www.goodreads.com/author/list/21997660.James_Bonk)

- Facebook (search '*James Bonk Author*' or go here: https://www.facebook.com/people/James-Bonk-Author/100092204034685/)

- BookBub (https://www.bookbub.com/profile/james-bonk)

The Author -
James Bonk